ALONG COME THE SUN

GEORGE ZAMALEA

INDIA • SINGAPORE • MALAYSIA

ISBN 979-8-89066-999-5

This book is dedicated to

Mythis, Jeremy

Jorgito and Knighton –

who have taught me how to genuinely patience

is

and listen is part of growth

and

Mailee

and all who love them.

Contents

Author's Note — vii
Acknowledgments — ix
Cast of Characters — xi

Chapter 1 — 1
Chapter 2 — 23
Chapter 3 — 28
Chapter 4 — 30
Chapter 5 — 31
Chapter 6 — 33
Chapter 7 — 35
Chapter 8 — 37
Chapter 9 — 38
Chapter 10 — 40
Chapter 11 — 42
Chapter 12 — 44
Chapter 13 — 46
Chapter 14 — 48
Chapter 15 — 50
Chapter 16 — 52
Chapter 17 — 55
Chapter 18 — 56
Chapter 19 — 58
Chapter 20 — 60
Chapter 21 — 63
Chapter 22 — 65
Chapter 23 — 66
Chapter 24 — 70
Chapter 25 — 72

Chapter 26 76
Chapter 27 81
Chapter 28 87
Chapter 29 89
Chapter 30 91
Chapter 31 100
Chapter 32 102
Chapter 33 103
Chapter 34 108
Chapter 35 109
Chapter 36 110
Chapter 37 111
Chapter 38 113
Chapter 39 115
Chapter 40 117
Chapter 41 123
Chapter 42 127
Chapter 43 132
Chapter 44 136
Chapter 45 139
Chapter 46 146
Chapter 47 150
Chapter 48 157
Chapter 49 164
Chapter 50 173
Chapter 51 175
Chapter 52 179
Chapter 53 181
Chapter 54 196
Chapter 55 208
Chapter 56 216

Author's Note

All of the voices contained in this book are derived from my ongoing *The Banana Republican's* research project. However, names, places, and other details contained in these material have been altered to protect the privacy and anonymity of the individuals to whom they refer. Therefore, any similarity between the names and stories of individuals described in this book and those of individuals known to readers is inadverted and purely coincidental.

Acknowledgments

I would thus like to take this brief opportunity to offer my gratitude to some of the people who helped make *Alone Come the Sun* possible.

First, I would like to thank Yashaswini S, the publishing manager, whose sharpen eyes patience, energy, and the editing ability were essential to the making of this book; and Diya Chandhok, in connection to the first amender, went through my work and her editorial suggestions are reflective of the highest order of settled the final visualization of the story.

And other staff at Notion Press Media Pvt Ltd have also been unceasingly supportive, and I thank you as well, and friends, Oscar, William, and Lizanille – all of you I thank you.

Cast of Characters

William "Rocko" Rockefeller Junior

Aram "Ares" Agdain

Abdiel "Ab" or "But" Butcher

Gilbert "Gil" Ramirez

Solito "Sol" Kuo

Tommy "Popo" Popovic

Kank "Al" Aldridge

Greg "Big" Cruz

Jeff "Jet" Jerssen

Mel "Eyes" Fafar

Etmo "Witz" Markowitz

Don "Lagi" Lagaspi

Phil "Patel" Patterson

Bruce "Ha" Hanlon

And Other Kids

Colonel Ruth Canon de Mposi

Assistant Sandhu

Cook Renita Borzaga (Melanie Leyva)

Sue, daughter

Master Chiefs

Rudolph Guerra (Steven McGowan)

Ranjit Sandhu

Josh Hansel

Miguel Bojorguez

Dieng Chung

Joe Mendoza

Alfredo Izmatch

Quillermo Hurtado

Brian Habert

Yokata Metlow

And Others

Chapter 1

I could not stand my father. This unscrupulous man who dared to love a dead fly more than a human being. Somehow, I was dependent on him. I needed him as he needed me. Both of us seemed to be attached to each other by an invisible chain. I carried his name and I was the only one to do so. I was Rockefeller Junior and the first son of his first marriage. I was a spoiled son and very unpredictable, an awkward, moody, compulsive young fellow. How many children ever really came to such a realization on their own? In my experience, none. Even though I had five brothers and three sisters—one of whom I loved—from his second and third marriages, I was a strange creature to them. They did not exist to me.

I was standing in front of his mahogany desk. He was an extraordinary man. He brought power and prestige to anything he touched. At 68, he was remarkably healthy. Trim. His chest big as a bull's. Forest-green eyes. He was beyond any rules. An old, good-looking man who was still admired by women and men alike. He was smart and merciless. A banker who managed his hundred employees with an iron fist and demanded to see them lined up in the large hall of the Cotus Building Enterprise every morning upon his arrival. They had to call him Mr. Rockefeller. It occurred to me that somehow I had the same halo he did and what I got from his paternal behavior was that he had a different approach towards me, not one of hatred but one designed to teach me responsibility, to carry his legacy when he would be gone. Instead, I did whatever I pleased, the only one in the family to do so.

My father changed position and put aside the notes he was reading. He raised his head and focused his eyes on my face.

"I've all the records from Harvard. By the time you reach your third year, you will be nothing."

"My mother's death seems to have affected me, Dad."

"It has been three years. Before that, you were struggling and scrubbing for recognition. You shall not put your dead mother in front of me as an excuse. I will not allow that. Don't you understand?"

I was busy looking out the window. The day was good for fishing in the waters of the Bahamas or racing in the Holy Land of the Rockville Rampart with my friends. This was what I had been thinking about since the morning.

I heard his hand come thudding down on the table.

"Are you paying attention to what I am saying to you, William?"

I peered into his eyes. There was a competition to see who could last longer. Who dared to turn? I did. Next time, I was going to win.

"Dad?"

"Stop it! I don't know what my options are with you, William. You are failing and soon I am going to bury you."

"As I said, my mother's death."

He stood.

His gigantic figure dwarfed me. Each vein of his body appeared to be exploding. His eyes were on me. "You dare to insult me again, you are going to bleed, William."

There was a pause.

That was the first time I heard it. I took my chance. I repeated what was in my head. It was my mother's death. My dad's arm stretched out, and then his open hand reached my face and sent me several feet from his desk, and I judged him with pain and hatred in my eyes. I glanced at my right hand when I touched my lips. It was covered with blood. I hurried to square my knees on the wooden floor. He was there. He lifted me up and stared at me. His eyes were darker. However, his voice was calmer, lower; he was whispering, as his anger appeared to have settled.

"I don't care what you are going to do, William," he said. "But I swear on Jesus Christ, you are going to make me happy and be a man. I don't have the patience of your mother. I don't. And I don't approve of your long parties and drinking, but there is a woman who needs a man and a doctor."

"Father!"

"Shut up, William!" He squeezed me against him. "She is the last of the Fords, and she is living in Tropical Island, and you will leave tomorrow to meet your future wife."

"What about Harvard, Father?"

"I have decided you are going to another school overseas, where your course will alternate between assignments and long hours of outdoor working."

He freed me and pushed me away from him. I did not understand what he was saying. A woman. Working. Outdoors. In a place I did not know about. It seemed an illusory world I had not visited yet.

"If I refuse it, what will happen then?"

He turned and looked at me. "I'll cut you off, William."

After some minutes, he let me go. Outside his office, I yelled. My father's employees at Leading Estate Corp. glanced at me. I cursed them. With remarkable calm, I moved out of the building. My chauffeur, Randal Harris, came out of the Rolls Royce. He looked at me.

"Where are you going, Junior? You've three days left."

"I've changed my mind. Take me to Rockefeller Airport. And please, get me Ernest. When you have done that, please tell Mr. Calkar to ready the jet."

I sat in the back seat of the Roll Royce. I was thinking. I recognized that this step I was going to take would distance me more from my father. I was going to see if I was really his son.

"Ernest is on the telephone, sir."

I pressed the buzzer. "Where are you calling me from, Will?"

"Do you want to eat breakfast in the Bahamas?"

"Red fish. I hate French toast."

"You will have red fish."

"Have you thought about any girls?"

"I haven't. If you have some who know how to have fun and are irresponsible, they are welcome. Otherwise, you come alone."

"In fact, I do have some, Will. Where do I meet you?"

"At my father's airport."

I smirked. Life was good and I had to respect it. While the Rolls was moving, I was ready to break another rule, adding it to the many I had broken before. I caught myself staring at my red face. I was a handsome young man. Rich and open-minded. I was 16 and I didn't have a dream or future. I was born with money on both sides—from my mum and dad—and, no matter what my dad said, I was his son. It suited me well enough to not give a damn what he thought of me. Sometimes it seemed I had never suffered. I didn't cry when my mother died. I accepted mum's death as a natural part of life. I missed her, of course, as that was part of being her favorite son. Her love was unquestionable. Tender. So precise and matter-of-fact that it was pure. She died of cancer. That was the reason I hated God and Dad. Everyone at Hyde Estate cried for her, including the iron man by the name of Walter Steinberg Rockefeller.

Before a massive door on which "Rockefeller Jets" was painted in white, the black Rolls Royce smoothly glided to a stop. I left the car. I stretched out my arms, took a deep breath, and smelled the air. The morning was blue and cool. I thought the ocean would be better. At this moment, Ernest's 2000 Vector Avtech reached the private parking lot and stopped noisily. He jumped out of the car without opening the driver's door. He was a good buddy. Few of my friends could match him. He was a rich son. Tall, fit, and absolutely irresponsible. He had a sense of royalty and respect for those who shared his views about the world around him. The earliest memories I had of Ernest's father were of the man's unchecked brutality, though I was merely repeating what he had told me about his father. I think he was all for his mother. I could not help but say he was a mother's boy.

"Where are the girls?"

"They are coming!"

First was Judith. An American beauty. She was the daughter of Mr. Grant Rosborough, the giant mind behind Microsoft Orc in England, Canada, and Australia. A sweet angel and a well-made-up blonde. She wore a sexy European faux leather corset-style top with lace and spaghetti straps, showing her virginal breasts, and a very short skintight fit skirt, the kind of outfit only Parisian girls dared to wear. She kissed Ernest, with whom she had a platonic relationship, since they had both been at St. Castillo-Sally Catholic School fifteen years earlier. She looked at me. "William? It's a pleasure. Ernest has spoken about you lots."

"Not in a favorable way, I hope."

I stared at her. Her sensuous breasts and the astonishing beauty of her face made me wonder if she was real. She didn't seem to mind when I said that, so I finished my observation and I perceived she was indeed a stunning American girl.

Her friend was next to her. Priscilla. We admired her new Lamborghini, imported directly from Italy. Ernest introduced her to me. He thought she would be my first choice for tonight. My mind hadn't changed. So we would see. She was an attractive young girl. Intelligent. She wanted to work for NASA. Her mother, Catherine Kipple, the last heir of John Kipple, the oil magnate of Gulf Inc., could not understand her daughter's choice. Priscilla had lost her father when she was only five. He had left her a fortune of $3 billion, which her mother had multiplied by marrying the old man Mr. Homs, a real estate icon. She was slender and I observed she had a good sense of humor.

A 1997 Classic Panox followed a Ferrari F-50. All of us had to jump to avoid broken bones. Ann got out of her Panox. Right away, she hit me with her sexuality and the easy movements of her body. She was a gorgeous young American Jew. Her hair was long. I noticed she had a tattoo across her belly, which made her very desirable.

We saluted her just as Meredith's Ferrari made us jump to the right, and all of us rolled left in panic.

"Jesus!"

"You crazy girl!"

"Damn!"

"I thought it was me driving!"

She was laughing with gusto. Short hair, and dressed like a 1960s hippy rock star—a Woodstock-inspired fringe top, tie-dye head band that seemed to be a part of her long red hair, sunglasses, a pair of torn bleached jeans showing her soft white skin off, but underneath that nonsense mask of unkemptness, she was indeed a beauteous girl. She was exceptionally sexy and vulnerable in some way. I introduced myself. Among them, I was the richest, followed by Judith, Ernest, Ann and Meredith.

We moved to the jetliner and, in a few minutes, we were in the air and flying to the Bahamas. We began drinking cognac and smoking. Ann produced a golden box filled with blue pills and she told us they were a new drug many of her friends were using in her private school, and they imparted feelings of euphoric omnipotence. Each one of us had one, and right away we started feeling good. Clouds became the faces of birds, and at the same time we noticed those clouds turned out to be monsters making funny faces. The blue sky was now a pool of butterflies and it kept changing. Even God was beautiful and still.

The jetliner was now in the middle of the ocean and I could remember the first time I had looked at the sea on the last trip I had taken with my mother when she was alive. It was fascinating, especially so because of how stoned as I was, bewitched by the drugs and alcohol. The panoramic view was drop-dead gorgeous. The blue water was deep. I could see the fishes swimming under the water. I saw myself down there. I was swimming among the fishes. "Damn, guys! This shit is good," I heard myself say. My feelings echoed. All of us were laughing. The girls were high and happy. I called Greg Vaughan, one of the Rockefeller family servants, but he didn't pick up. An hour later, I tried the house again and spoke with Mr. Canales.

"Is it you, Junior?"

"Yes, Mr. Canales. Wait for me at the Landing Rockville."

"Are you coming to the island?"

"Yes, Mr. Canales."

"No one has told me about your visit, sir. None of the servants are here."

"It does not matter. I will not need them."

"Are you coming alone?"

"No. With friends."

"Very well, sir. I will send my son."

"Great, Mr. Canales. Please, don't say a word to dad."

"No. I will not."

Hours later, the jetliner yielded altitude, sweeping over the high canopy of the coconut forest. As the jetliner moved towards the private landing strip, we saw the natives waving at the plane. I thought I was going to have a good time. By the time the plane landed on the Rockefeller Landing Rockville field, the thought of Shawn, whom my father had told me to marry, was gone.

At the Landing, Canales' son, Verdis, was standing beside an English SUV. He was a brawny young man, muscled and handsome. Meredith quickly had her eye on him.

We were excited and high. The tropical weather and the sun reinforced us with a kind of magic excitement. So far, we had swallowed three pills more. We climbed into the SUV. An hour later, Verdis was driving along a narrow pathway near the Canyon.

"Can you go faster, Verdis?" Ann said, trying to take the wheel from Verdis.

"It will be impossible, Miss. A mistake and we will all fall below the cliff."

"None will fall." She crossed one of her legs over the driver's seat. All of us saw her Brazilian panties. She smiled. Verdis was smiling but he was very cautious about not letting her take over the wheel. Judith held Ann back and fell on Priscilla. She jumped but Judith tried to push Verdis aside. The SUV lost balance, hitting rocks, but he was capable of controlling the vehicle.

"Be careful!"

We laughed.

I sent Judith and Ann to the back, where Ernest was, and I pressed Verdis' foot. The vehicle jumped ahead.

"No, Junior! You don't know these pathways the way I know them. Remember that day!"

He was talking about a day I did not remember. So I kept pressing his foot. Ernest was amongst Ann and Meredith, who was laughing.

But then came the impact. Among us, someone said, "It's a pig, isn't it?"

"A pig!"

Before the Rockefeller farmhouse, I used my foot to brake. All of us were hurled forward. There was a loud sound in the car. Ernest's head hit the back of my passenger seat. "Damn it, William!"

We laughed.

"Hey! Come in! We have to change." I moved, along with Verdis, who was looking at us. He was shaking but he could not say a word to a Rockefeller. He shook his head. I put my hand on his shoulder. He was a lucky one. Meredith leaned over and kissed one of his cheeks.

"You're born a man. I like that. *Me gusta mucho, ¿sí?*"

"Prepare the yacht. We are going to have our breakfast in the ocean."

"I will tell Mr. Thomas, Junior."

Meredith came over to me and whispered. "Tell him to come."

"Did you hear, Verdis?"

"No, Junior. What is it?"

"Meredith wants you to come with us."

"Oh. Thank you, Miss Woodard."

I ran into the house and saluted Mrs. Canales and Mr. Canales, the housekeepers of the Great Casa. I moved along the corridor as I showed the rooms to Ernest and the girls.

"Will your clothes fit me, William?"

"You are not going to a cocktail party, Ernest! For God's sake, man!"

"I know we go to the sea. Well, suppose I find there a siren, and she invites me to see her folks below, uh?"

I laughed. The girls did, too.

"You will be a lucky man."

"What about us?" Judith asked.

"All the clothes of my sisters are there. Some untouched."

"Are they sexy clothes?"

"Never ask."

"Have you seen them naked, William?"

Judith stared at me across the hallway expecting a reply from me. I told her I had seen them naked, especially Frances.

She had small breasts and they were quite provocative. She was still a virgin and fetching. I tried to speak to her about the other sister, but she had already moved with Meredith to the room. I stayed where I was, and I had an inkling of the reason she had asked me that question. Watching them peer at the walk-in closet, I admired the two girls. I let my mind wander while Judith and Meredith were selecting bikinis. Judith turned and looked at me. Both women began teasing me.

"Are you ready to see me naked, William?"

I did not reply. By that time, Meredith had turned and was studying me.

I stretched my right arm and pulled the door close.

At the pier, the yacht was on the water. It was a remarkable bright, blue day. Verdis made the last preparations and we moved in.

Obviously, the weather was perfect. Ernest and I were thinking of making the best of it. The yacht entered the deep water. A few minutes later, the girls came out of the rooms. Ann was wearing a classic bikini that she had found among my other sister Suzan's belongings, and it fit her perfectly. She found a good spot in the corner of the yacht and looked at the sea. Priscilla had a Rio brief, and she had let her hair cascade over her shoulders. Judith made her appearance. She had on a low-rise V-string. I realized she was the most graceful girl I had ever seen. Meredith was unable to find anything for herself, but she was all right with her Victory's Secret plunge. She had worn it for Verdis.

After a moment, they came together in the middle of the yacht. All the girls lay there and started talking and smoking amongst themselves. Verdis captained the yacht; he, too, was admiring the girls, especially Meredith. Ernest looked at me carrying the casting rod with handles and all the preparations for fishing.

"You should not take it personally," he said, "but what Meredith is doing to that native is unfair. That's seduction, real seduction, unconditional, self-esteem-taking seduction. I warn you."

"I don't see that, Ernest. He is a servant. She will have him only for that teen fancy of power."

"Are you going to have Judith instead? She can be a line roller when you decide to jump over her."

I looked in her direction. I pictured myself with her in a remote place in the universe called Trist, a planet for rich and famous teens, where I started kissing those voluptuous lips of hers and at the same time playing with her long hair. She was in the middle of the group. Also, I took a look at Meredith. I understood why Ernest had said what he had said about her. Meredith was indeed a teaser, lying across Ann, showing off her beauty to Verdis; her camel-toe was quite marked. There was no romance here, I thought. The girls were here for us; the only thing I was thinking about was whether to have Judith or Meredith; but I was sure Judith would be the one I desired more. What was the complication here? I think it was the most blind, most faithful form of power. Or that was my arrogance. Verdis was just a native, and I was his employer. I doubted he had forgotten his place before my authority. If I told him to jump in the water, there was no doubt he would. Both of them, Meredith and him, were mine if I decided so.

"You've all of what we're looking for." Ernest said, opening the buzzbaits, and selected one. "I hope he knows how to cook my fish."

I signaled to Verdis to stop the yacht. He did but he kept watching the girls, who knew they were teasing him. The girls got to their feet. I yelled at him.

"Hey, Verdis! You pay attention to what you are doing."

"Yes, Junior."

"Are you alright, Will?" Meredith asked.

"Yes. I am fine."

"We are going to swim."

"I thought we were going to do it after we caught some fish."

"You should."

Ernest looked at me. I stood there holding the cranking combo. I saw Judith move to the edge of the yacht.

"The water is remarkably blue."

I called Verdis and commanded him to catch some fish.

"I thought he would come with us."

"He's just an employee, Meredith. We need him here."

She glanced at Ernest and then at me. "I came here to have fun, Will, not to make anyone uncomfortable."

"You would have more fun if you did not mix business with pleasure, Meredith."

The girls and Ernest looked at me. I had tried to make that observation a joke, but I had said it very seriously.

Judith waved to Priscilla. She ran and jumped into the water. She was followed by Ann and Meredith. Ernest yelled, and I echoed him. Both of us splashed into the water.

The water was very warm. We moved deep and it was warmer. Each one of us was very good in the water. I moved first with Ernest and then with Judith when Priscilla sought his company. It was quite easy swimming with Judith. She dared to go deep, making me follow her. She was a rebel. But she had found a rebel in me, too, and she wanted to challenge me. I would not take it. I needed to be only me. Moving away from the yacht, we explored the sea bottom. While we were swimming, I could not help but see her body from below, as I was really in a mood to hold her. She was naked. But Judith's daring made me feel strong. She disappeared through the shadowy water. I followed. Below, I saw a band of jaws. I sighed. She swept towards me and pressed her body against mine. Then, slowly, we moved back. The rest of the girls and Ernest were waiting for us. Judith did not change. She climbed the yacht as she was, naked.

"The native boy has caught some fish and he is cooking them."

I nodded. I did not see Meredith around, but Judith's beauty made me forget her for a while. I sat on the water sofa. I was watching her as Ernest moved towards Ann and Priscilla. Both girls were kissing. I got up and moved to Judith. She lay on her back. For a moment, she opened her eyes.

"I want to feel high."

"Ernest has some Jamaican joints. We will have them after we eat."

"I am talking about Meredith's blue pills."

"Ann, do you know where Meredith's blue pills are?"

"They're gone."

"So fast?"

"I've marihuana. "

"I told Judith that we would have it after eating." I looked at her. I put my hand over her shoulder and ran it over her breasts.

"Well, bring it and let us smoke."

Ernest got up and moved to the corner of the yacht. He brought back a bag of weed and quickly made five homemade cigars. He lit one and gave it to me. Then he lit another and moved back to Ann and Priscilla.

Judith passed the cigar. "I thought you'd take Meredith first."

"How did you figure it out, Ermest?"

"The way you have been looking at her. She's a great teaser. I think that native will get the wrong ideas from what she is doing."

She looked at the cabin and pressed her body into mine. After a moment, she turned and peeped at me. "I don't mind, Mr. William Rockefeller, Jr. I can be the last or the first. I don't care." She swept aside the wet hair that covered her eyes and tilted her head back. "Do you want me, William?"

As I was about to reply, I and the others heard a scream coming from inside the yacht. We turned. Meredith was coming out with an expression of fear.

"What happened?" Ann asked over Ernest with an air of pleasant relaxation.

"That animal!"

"What?"

Verdis appeared, holding his shorts.

"Oh, my God!" Priscilla exclaimed.

We got up. A thrill of anger swept through me.

"What did you do, you savage?"

"Nothing, Junior. It was her."

"You bastard! You don't know how to play safe!"

I didn't realize I was in front of him. I began to beat him. But he was a seasoned and strong young man. Soon there was a fight. I had learned a series of martial art techniques and

I wondered if I could beat him. It became ugly. Verdis was not afraid that I was a Rockefeller boy. I realized it couldn't be an ordinary fight. Two boys fighting on the campus of a high school was fine. This was not a high school match and Verdis was not a student. I remembered that nobody had hit me before and rage overtook me. I heard voices and sounds around us. I was an animal. Verdis and I wrestled in the middle of the yacht, falling, while we wrangled to get the best of each other. I grasped a rod. I showed every sign of madness. I had entered a level of no return. I was blind. I hammered the rod into something hard and Verdis' skull opened. I heard screams from somewhere. Something breaking. A splash.

"Oh God! Meredith is in the water!"

I heard more voices. I heard Ann's voice as I felt someone pulling me.

And then everything stopped.

I sat on the floor. I noticed first a bloody body several feet from me. It was Verdis. He was dead. I turned around and whispered, "What happened?"

Ann was beside Judith and she seemed to be helping her. And I saw she was bleeding. "Where is Ernest? Ernest? Ernest?"

He appeared. He moved around, trying to find something. I looked at him.

"You must be with me, Will. All right?"

"Tell me, Ernest. He isn't dead, is he?"

"He is dead, but there is more, William."

I got to my feet and saw my blood and thought I was hurt. "I didn't mean that."

"I want you to focus, William. We've lost Meredith and Priscilla. They fell into the water while you were fighting with him."

"But how?"

"It does not matter how, William. I'll take this yacht to where they fell."

"We must call the police, Ernest. We've a dead body here and Meredith and Priscilla have fallen in the water."

"Please calm down, Ann. How is Judith?"

"In pain."

I looked around. I saw Verdis. He lay there. His head crushed. A wire across his face.

"William, help me move the yacht back there."

Obviously, we didn't know how to do this. We tried. We were able to turn to the yacht toward the place where he presumed the girls had fallen in the water, and Ernest indicated to me the flag he had thrown previously into the water.

"There, William!"

We passed the flag because we were unable to stop the yacht in time. We moved the yacht back, heard its engine rumble, and were finally able to hold it still.

We began to examine the water, but we found nothing.

"I need to get down there."

"Will you be able to handle it, William?"

Ann and Judith, who was bleeding from her face, approached us.

"What are you going to do, Ernest?"

"Get down there. I'm wondering if I can find them."

"How? They might be dead by now."

"I have to."

"We should call the police. They will be here within minutes."

"We're going to handle the police later on, Ann."

"I don't know why you reached the level of killing, William."

"Cut it off, Ann," Ernest snapped.

I looked at her angrily. "You heard what he did to Meredith."

"None of us knows if he raped her or not, William. If that's what you're referring to."

"Goddamn you, Ann! Shut the fuck up and go there and take care of Judith!"

I was letting out my last reserves of anger. I glanced at Judith, and she did not say anything. I perceived her pain across her face, and now I recalled that she had tried to stop my fight with Verdis.

Ernest found the waders. Without any protection for his eyes, he jumped into the water. Hours passed. It was a long and terrifying spell of waiting. Finally, he emerged several feet from the left side of the yacht. He waved at us and then went into deep water once again. Suddenly, after several minutes, he emerged. This time he was not alone. We watched him as he pulled one of the girls, and I was wondering if he would make it.

"Do something, William!"

I thought about our safety boat. It was a way to bring back Ernest and the person he was pulling with him to the yacht. I released the boat and it splashed into the water. We began to scream. I threw a rope. Ernest finally grasped the boat. There was a yell. Ann and I began to pull on the rope. We saw now that one of Priscilla's legs was gone.

"Oh, mercy!"

"William, hold the rope firmly. I need to load Priscilla in."

We did it. We pulled Priscilla's body out of the water. Yes. Her right leg was chopped off close to her waist. "Meredith must be there, too. In this part of the sea."

"She could have experienced the same or worse."

"I need to go back there."

"Soon the sun will be gone."

"I am going to call for help." Ann started to move to the cabin to make the call.

I held her and slapped her face. "Don't!"

"Don't you dare do that again, William! Do you hear me? Sick bastard!"

"No police!" I hit her again.

"Shit!"

"William! William!" Ernest pulled me off her. I crashed into the wall of the yacht. There was pain inside me. I think that part of me was broken or something.

"Fuck!"

"You stay there, William, hear me?"

"She wants to call the police. We should not allow it."

"Damn you, Will! I want you to focus, man! Got me?"

"She is going to call the police."

"Eventually we need to call the police whether like you or not. We need to report what's happened here."

"I'll be in trouble, Ernest. There are two dead bodies here and a missing person."

"Hey, William! We are rich boys! Our daddies can fix it, hear me?"

"We need to clean this mess and throw Verdis' body into the ocean."

"Give me a chance to find Meredith."

"Yes! Yes!"

"Stay with me, Will."

I began creating a scenario. They were swimming ... an incident ... a big fish ... her leg gone ...

"Let me see, okay, Will?"

"That is insane! Are you listening to yourselves? It's murder! You're talking about murder."

"Stop it, Ann! Please!"

Planning what we were going to do, I saw Ernest pace around. He was active and very cool, giving instructions to Ann to look after Judith. After a moment, he jumped into the water and disappeared. I ambled to the bow of the yacht. Hours passed. Ernest emerged several times and finally came back to the yacht. He was exhausted.

As he was explaining the new situation to us, we heard a siren. It was a police boat from the Bahamas. I turned and I tried to find Ann. I found her standing behind the wheel.

"You bitch! We need to throw the body into the water!"

"No!"

I looked at Ernest, but jerked back and ran toward Verdis' body. I lifted him and tossed him overboard.

"What have you done? You fool!" Ann screamed.

The boat arrived and the police stepped onto our yacht.

"Hey! We received a call from the Rockefeller residence. Is everything all right here?"

A brawny athletic police officer of the Bahamas was staring at us.

"A call?"

He nodded towards Ernest, and he began examining the yacht. Immediately, he noticed the blood and the mess on the yacht. I realized that Ann had not made the call. It had come from the estate. Ernest began explaining the situation of the yacht to the second policeman, but I did not reply when he wanted me to corroborate what Ernest was saying. I had my own story, and I made Ernest look stupid.

"We were swimming and having a good time when a big fish began to attack us. She lost her leg and Ernest saved her. Meredith is still missing and our captain Verdis is as well."

I talked more, creating a new scenario in which all actions were linked. I looked at Ernest and the girls. Their eyes were glued to the floor. Police officer Oscar Rankins took notes and whispered something to his partner, Dorothy Crispen. I saw him looking at Priscilla and the site where Verdis had fallen. The blood—there was a lot of it. The knife was there. I could not pick it up fast enough. He saw the broken rod and the brass gear covered with blood. He did not ask questions. He knew all of us aboard the yacht belonged to rich parents.

Help arrived—another police boat and a helicopter. The divers jumped into the water. We decided to stick to my first story. Hours later, they found Verdis. Untouched. I remembered I had told the police about the Jaws-style attack, realizing then that it would seem bizarre when they saw his head opened up and the wounds on his body. Still, none of them questioned us. Somehow, I couldn't help feeling a bit nervous, because I thought they would naturally discover that someone among us was lying. Three persons had died and I still had the sense that eventually they were going to discover the truth.

Anyhow, in a few hours, they found Meredith several miles north, far away from where Ernest was looking for her. She was awfully pale, but she was intact, except for the hole in her forehead. I presumed that had happened when she was trying to separate Verdis and me. She might have been pushed to the edge of the deck, where she hit her forehead and then fell into the water. The police officers took notes about everything. They made no remarks, as though the stories and the scenarios I had told them did not match what they were seeing. To me, all that I had said made perfect sense. Besides, our lawyer would figure it out.

The police officer named Oscar stepped into the cabin and looked at each one of us. He made some comments that I did not care about. "What really happened, Mr. Rockefeller?"

"What have I told you, sir?"

He had large and steady eyes, almost immobile, dead. They were very light brown and tense. They were unquestionably sexy. "I have to call your parents."

"You don't believe our story?"

"To be honest, Mr. Rockefeller, I don't."

"That's too bad."

"Yeah. It's too bad."

Chapter 2

Hours later, without changing our clothes, hungry and tired, we were all in a big room. Its air was hot like an oven. There was no air conditioning or windows and it made us miserable and irritable. They served us homemade meals and coconut water in such small quantities that a minute later we were still hungry. Our fathers and mothers were rich and eventually all these problems would be gone. It had all been an accident. Drugs, alcohol, and those things could be explained. Now we ate and waited. We didn't talk. I tried to speak with Judith, but she did not reply when I asked her how she felt. She was thinking. Ernest was quiet, squeezing his hands while hoping to escape. Ann was silent and apart from us. Priscilla was missing and we did not hear a word from the police officers. There was a call for Ann. The door opened and a police officer took her out. One by one, they called each of us. The same question: "What happened on the yacht?"

When they called me, I told Ernest we had to stick to the story I had made up. I expected to be interrogated not by a policeman but by my father. Instead, I found the police officers from the yacht. There were five of them. I refused to answer their questions. I told them, "I am a Rockefeller and I need my father here."

"We know that, Mr. Rockefeller."

"Then why am I here and why all of these questions?" I said. "I told you guys what happened."

They sent me back to the room without replying. I called them names. I screamed that I was an American teen and a minor and our Constitution required that they provide me with a lawyer and what they had been doing was abuse under the American flag. The girls and Ernest asked me how it had been. I did not reply. I felt pain in my back and sides. I lay on the floor and tried to get some sleep.

When I woke up, it was because one of the Rockefeller family lawyers was there. He said his name was Greg Katz. He was unknown to me. I wondered where David Packer, Lou Mitchell, and Luis Martinez, Jr. were. I did not really care about the lawyer's name. I had spent five days in that filthy room, and my friends and I were tired. I began to talk about the treatment we were receiving. He did not interrupt me. He listened to the stories and the scenarios I had painted.

"Mr. Rockefeller, Jr. They have a different version of what you are telling me."

"What?" Looking at him and breathed heavily, I said, "What they have is nothing. Jesus! Are you going to believe those uncivilized people or me? For Mary's feet! What side are you on, sir?"

"Please, tell me what really happened?"

I turned my head and my whole body as well. I disliked being questioned about anything. So I tried to be calm, but Greg Katz did not care. He had a job to do and there was a lot of money he had already received from my father. I began to talk, describing everything from the moment that Meredith came out from inside the yacht. Mr. Katz objected to my use of the word "rape."

"She was not raped by Verdis, Mr. Rockefeller, please! They already have examined her and there was no indication of force entry."

"How could they? She was in the water!"

"She had been examined by the doctors of the island and they noticed she was not raped by him as you appeared to state. Besides, our specialists have confirmed the previous report and the latest ones."

"Bullshit!" I exclaimed. "How did she fall in the water anyway?"

"When you were fighting with Verdis, Meredith was trying to separate you two. You turned and hit her on her forehead."

"That's a lie!"

"They have witnesses."

"Who? Ann? She doesn't know a thing."

"They have heard it all from Ernest."

This shocked me. Not Judith, of course, but Ernest.

"I want to see my father."

"I need your side of the story, Mr. Rockefeller. It will be the only thing that can save you."

"I want to see my father. Hear me?"

"It is impossible. He is in London."

"Call him. Tell him where I am."

"That is why I am here, isn't it?"

I slammed the palm of my hand on the surface of the table as my daddy had done when he was angry. "I want you to call my father. Now!"

"I don't work for you, Mr. Rockefeller."

"You work for me because I am a Rockefeller."

"No, sir! I am working for Rockefeller Senior."

"You're going to be punished. Hear me?"

"I will not!"

Slowly, I began to tell the story from a different perspective, not caring about whether Judith or Ann or Ernest were implicated along the way. While I was telling him the second made-up story, Mr. Katz was writing my words down. It took me a few minutes. A moment later, I told him I wanted to speak with my father.

"Again, you cannot speak with him at this moment."

"Is he in London?"

"That's what Cornie Blackwell told me, yes."

I didn't think he was in London. I thought I would call him and explain to him all that had happened to me over the telephone. The door opened and the man was there, his face shaven and smelling of snowball cologne for men, the one mom would buy for him. When he stepped in, I got up. I indicated a chair to him, but he refused to sit.

"I haven't come here to make a long speech, William."

"You are not that man, Father."

"Certainly not. But you are my son and I refuse to give up all the things you may need. This must change, and I hope you learn from it." He turned and moved to the door. "Ten years will be a good lesson."

I stepped forward and I looked at him. "Father, I'm so sorry."

He halted for a moment and then turned. He stared at me, but now I was by myself and time was my companion and I did understand, and he recognized that a part of me had died forever.

"I am still your son and I think all I can do is depend on you."

"Yes, William. I can see it now."

"Father!"

"Your sister Frances is here. Do you want to speak with her?"

I thought about it. I moved to the window and saw her among my other sisters and brothers. There was a smile across my face.

"No, Father."

"They will take you to the local jail and three weeks from now they are going to bring you before a magistrate. Mr. Katz will be there, and I will, too. Would you want me to bring you something?"

"Who is that Ford girl?"

"Her name is Allyson."

"Can I get her telephone number?"

I saw a slight smile emerge across his stony face. "I can arrange it, William. I think your sister Frances will be able to bring it to you on her first visit."

"Thank you, Father. I love you."

He opened the door. He hesitated and then came over to me and embraced me. "I love you, too, son."

It took me a minute to grasp my dad's action, but then I abandoned myself in his arms.

"Dad."

"You take care of yourself now, son. I'll be behind you all the way."

He withdrew from me and moved to the door. This time, he didn't turn. He pulled the door open and stepped out. I felt empty as the door closed behind him. I didn't need to cry, but I did. When my body fell on the chair, it was the way I pitied myself that hurt me.

As I looked at Greg, I felt very bad. An illusion—I wished it was happening the way I have described it. But it was not.

It was more painful, more humiliating.

Chapter 3

There was no Greg Katz. No telephone or anything else that I could grasp. There was no visit from my father or my sister Frances or that Ford girl. It was all in my head as I tried to believe that they would come to cheer me up. You ask what was going on? I was trying to figure it out, too. No one would come and I was alone in this world of pain. They took me back to the sweltering room.

Judith had removed her sexy jacket and laid it next to her. Ann was staring at the wall. Ernest had lost all his confidence as a macho young man. I did not know what the time was when they called me again. I thought it was a quarter to five or two when they called me back to the other room asked me if I wanted to change my story. I wasn't sure.

No! I was not losing my goddamn mind. I was here before in this. The faces were different. A fat police officer was sitting behind a desk. He was fanning himself with an old lady's fan and smoking a black cigar. He blew the gray smoke into my face. I protected myself. He laughed. I cursed at him. He slapped my face.

"No bad words here."

"Don't hit me, okay?"

"Whatever! Now speak up. What happened on the yacht?"

"I told you I need a lawyer."

"Suit yourself."

He reached for a pencil and signed his name below mine. He shouted a name and a pair of guards strolled in.

"Take him away!"

"Where are you taking met? You need to call my father. Don't touch me!"

They did not listen. Ungraciously, they pulled my chair out and they gripped my shoulders and arms and dragged me out of the office. I struggled with them, mentioning human rights, international law and police brutality conventions. I kicked the floor and I held myself against the wall, but they managed to lift me up and separate me from the wall. In a new room, they subjected me to a series of punches.

"You're going to court Monday morning, babyface."

"Hey! Hey!"

They closed the door before me.

I turned. I tried to find Ernest, Judith or Ann. I found no one.

Chapter 4

I don't want my readers to think this is a horror story or a rabbit's hole gone bad. It is real and reality seemed to be beating me at every turn.

How did this happen? I was a rich boy and there was nothing wrong with being rich. That's life. I didn't kill anyone.

I was alone in the dirty room. I called Ernest and Judith and Ann. None of them replied to my call. I began to see the reality in all this. It was a joke, as if someone wanted to prank me. Father, no matter how mean he was, would not let this happen to me.

I called Ernest and the girls again.

"Ernest! Judith! Ann! C'mon, guys!"

This wasn't funny.

I didn't get it.

But I was supposed to get it already.

Chapter 5

They pulled me out of bed. I had been dreaming. I was driving my new sportscar from Saudi Arabia. I was drugged. I was happy. I was enjoying myself. A hand grabbed my face.

"You have three minutes to get ready, lazy pretty boy!"

I was still sleeping. The previous drugs had worn off. I had a terrible headache and I could not see well.

"Hey, I need to call my father."

"Usted no entiende, Señor Rockefeller."

"What? I don't speak Spanish."

That's too bad.

"Where is my breakfast?"

No breakfast.

"Well, let me call my father."

No overseas calls.

The short and bearded man pushed me against the wall and restrained me there. The other one put the handcuffs around my wrists.

"They are too tight!"

He pulled me with them and led me through a wet corridor to a pickup. He tossed me onto the back bed of the pickup.

I did not see Ernest, Judith or Ann. The pickup moved forward violently, and I almost fell. I was able to see streets, people and dogs. I found a dozen dogs digging into the street garbage and people pulling their vendor carts down along the dirty avenue and vendors carrying baskets on their shoulders and head. There were women, children and old people. Cars, carriages, wagons and bicyclists rushed down both sides of the narrow streets. The pickup did not reduce its speed over the holes of the street. I bounced up and down. The pickup sped across the plaza. It stopped noisily before a massive door. The police guard by the name of Bart Diener got out of the pickup. He pulled me out of the back bed of the pickup.

Chapter 6

They took me into a small room that they called a courtroom. The room was depressing, with ugly white walls and filled with morning flies, flying everywhere in the hot room, appearing to have fun in a strange way. There was a gigantic prematurely gray man behind a brown desk wearing a black robe with a bow tie in purple that did not match the cotton linen of the robe, and he tried to appear like a royal magistrate of the olden days, reading from a long legal document. He did not mention anything about where my lawyer was or whether someone was going to represent me. I spoke. Many times, he made me shut up and, if I did not, he had the authority to change his decision about my case.

What decision?

He stared at me over the rim of his heavy glasses. He had the ability to read the document at the same time, like a chameleon.

"Sir!"

"Can you understand what I say, boy? Shut up!"

"My lawyer must be here."

"You do not have a lawyer and no one will come. Besides that, we cannot afford any public defense for you."

"There has been a mistake."

"You just keep talking arrogantly, boy!"

I heard the judge say, "We the court."

The legal charges involved drugs, fornication, lack of values and morals, anti-social behavior, disrespect to other human beings and murder.

"Wait!"

"For God's sake! You must be quiet, young man!"

"I must talk, sire."

I began to act uncontrollably before him. The guards seized me, but I was still struggling with anger, trying to make the judge understand my situation, but the gloomy man, the so-called judge, wouldn't allow me to speak up. I felt a fist hit me, taking my breath away, and then the pressure of the handcuffs squeezing my wrists. Pain reached my brain directly, and they pulled my neck back.

"Now, you will be quiet!"

Chapter 7

A long list of legal charges related to the Verdis family suing William Rockefeller, Jr. and his family for wrongful death started to accumulate in front of me. They had said that I, William Rockefeller, Jr., had threatened the young man, Verdis Castano, and the *others*—that meant Ernest, Judith, Ann, Meredith and Priscilla—went along with the story that I had made up. Realizing that some information had been altered had upset me. I was ridiculed and declared ignorant when I brought up the fact that my father's lawyer was not in the courtroom with me. I was accused of killing intentionally. If I'd known that someone, Ernest or Judith, had been talking about me, I'd have said that all of them were liars. Of course, the judge would not allow my opinion in the court. But it was important to remember that the whole scenario that I had come up with had been staged by me to make things right for me. I could see that Ernest and the girls were probably acting to save their own skins. But if the readers accept what I tried to do, I think someday you will do something not great and comprehend that it was not my intention to kill Verdis or enact what happened to the girls. That declaration did not change when the judge hit me with the revelation that Verdis died due to negligence and not when he was fighting with me. I saw that Ernest and the girls had fucked me big time, even though I had trusted them.

When the action was initiated secretly in the Castano house family, and in Schumacher's office several weeks later when they brought me to the police station and then to this local judge by the name of Edward J. Kempner, I felt all hope was melting in front of me. He told me my case was one of biggest and most brutal of all the cases that had occurred on the island since 1990.

"Look at me, boy," he said huskily. "I charge you, Mr. Rockefeller, with attempting murder first degree by refusing to cooperate with the Island Authority and trying to hide your crime and denying any involvement in these murders and lying and using your name. This court is sentencing you to 40 years of hard labor."

"No! No!"

"The sentence shall run consecutively."

"No, goddamn you! Listen! There's been a mistake!"

"Take him away!"

Chapter 8

I wanted to know where I had failed. After one last look towards the judge, I felt devastated.

Would I take this humiliation of a Rockefeller?

Hell no!

I screamed at him. At all of them. I screamed with fear. With anger. Later on, I felt I had lost everything in front of this stony bovine man.

They removed me from the courtroom.

Outside the court building, people looked at me. I cursed them.

Dragging me to the pickup, they pushed me against the truck bed and restrained me there.

I felt no pain.

I felt nothing but humiliation.

Where was Dad? Where was Dad? I needed him!

Chapter 9

They awakened me in the middle of my dream. Blue sky. Blue water. I was flying over lovely scenes that one could only see in movies. They took me out of the jail cell. It was very early in the morning. The exact hour I did not know, but it was quite early.

I asked the tall and light-skinned jail guard where my friends Judith, Ann and Ernest were. The people they had brought with me. He did not reply as he was picking up my things, although there was almost nothing at all to pick up. My golden money holder, along with my phone, jewelry and money, had been taken away after they had brought me from the yacht.

I had just a soap bar, a toothbrush and a towel, but it did not matter.

I asked him the question with a "please," but he did not respond. I gave up.

In the lobby, they made me sign more than eleven sheets that were impossible to read because of the ink.

A police officer gave me a file with my name on it and led me out of the building.

Outside the station, the sky was darker. The streetlights were still on. Dogs and unwanted creatures were still rumbling down the alleys.

A truck was doubled parked in front of the station. A second man got out. He did not have any grace when he pulled me into the trunk bed and restrained me against it.

I tried to speak, to have a civilized conversation with them about where they would take me and where my friends were.

Silence.

I tried another approach to see if there was a possibility of sending a message to my dad.

"You must know my papa, brothers, and sisters. You must know that."

Nothing.

Then, suddenly, I heard one of them say, "Mposi. You goin' to Mposi."

"What was that? What do you mean? Mposi?"

Chapter 10

Mposi!

The name sent a chill down my spine.

Where was this place?

They did not tell me. It made me wonder if it was a place close to home or close to hell.

By the time fear seized me, the beefy man had driven twenty miles to the north, where a local airport was. I saw only three planes, and they were small, not commercial airplanes. I did not see any jetliners.

The driver stopped the truck and pulled me out.

A hunched man appeared from an inner office and strolled towards the men who had brought me. They exchanged words and papers. The Caribbean police officers turned and looked at him. They did not say a word as they got into the truck and drove away.

The hunched man glanced at me. He came over to me, grasped me by the handcuffs and led me to a small room within a tiny office.

"You will leave tomorrow. So don't get too comfortable."

"Oh, you can speak English!"

"Funny! Ha!"

"You should know I am an innocent young man and I am an American teenager."

"Who gives a shit!"

That was his reply. He backed up and closed the door. He looked around, found on the surface of the table a cold slice of pizza and a bottle of tamarind juice and deposited them on the floor in front of me.

I did not have any intention of picking them up. I was not a damned caged dog, but my situation showed no signs of changing. I picked them up, not knowing when I would have another opportunity to see food again, and I started eating.

Chapter 11

There was no railroad at Mahagan. There were no freeways, no main streets, restaurants, fast-food vendors, McDonald's outlets, or beach hot-dog vendors. It was not a place where people could have fun during spring break.

Everyone believed Mahagan in Brazil was a dead city that came before one reached a place called Mposi, deep in the forest of Brazil. If you dared to call it a living city, then you were on the wrong side of the Amazonian map.

It is just a narrow trail cut brutally between two hills. A sign, a name and an arrow indicated that Mposi Sugar Plantation was 300 kilometers to the south.

We changed our mode of transportation at Salima Coastal, a spot with colorful facades of trees, palms, and thick mountains—and hundreds of dangers. I noticed its inhabitants were trackers displaying across their chests their prices for particular jobs across the river or the jungle. I watched them gathering at the dreggy plaza. Negroes, creoles, natives and whites looking to do some hunting.

The British Mountain V-sport stopped at Bay Cannon. The handler man let me urinate right off the road and gave me a wrap with rice and beans and coconut water.

Hours later, when the horses later took us to Mposi, a new passage started to emerge. I noted we were deep in the forests of Brazil. Now it was a jungle. Green walls of trees and twisted roots.

So far, I was kind of surprised. Had they changed my sentence at the last minute? I hadn't seen mines and holes in the ground or caves, only the green vegetation of this astonishing and mysterious place.

I turned and looked at one of the hairy men wearing cowboy trousers, boots, a hat and the official badge of a police officer. He didn't look at me. He did not bother to answer what I asked him. Both of the officers appeared to be concentrating on where they were going.

There was no rest.

Hours passed. They ate and drank water from a container. They gave me some dried skin of pork and coconut water, but our horses kept galloping.

There was a shed built along the edge of the trail. They left the horses there. They helped me climb down from my horse. One of them examined my handcuffs. He loosened them a little, as the marks of the handcuffs had deepened on my delicate white skin.

I said nothing. I was a doomed dreamer.

We began to walk.

They warned me, "Watch out for the rarest insects!"

Chapter 12

"Mposi Sugar Plantation, 50 kilometers," the sign said, hanging on a tree.

The Oca Hut. It was built in 1890, and it had been abandoned since. One of my companions would not dare to move in. Instead, there was a cross telling wanderers to follow the blue rock. I hadn't seen any blue rock.

The blue rock was right in front of us. It was a rare blue rock and its rocky eye looked right into yours. There was a sign that said, "Do not look below."

I did.

One of the police officers caught me and brought me back to reality after I saw ghostly people riding on gigantic bugs below having a good time and calling me to join them.

"Stupid gringo!"

"They are not real!"

"Be quiet, boy!"

During my first term and during the rainy season, I made my first attempt to escape. I would venture north to this part, where I saw a river. Wrong way to come out of the jungle! If I had been taken south, I would have come out below Mahagan, where local legend has it that they ate teenagers like me. Everything was a mess after that. Indians took me and scared the hell out of me. I was therefore right there, where I had started. I blamed it on the rain, the fog, and not on anyone.

The news was that nobody had escaped from Mposi yet. No one. If they had some luck, they would never make it to the other side of the jungle.

Or, they said, the ethereal winds would carry them away.

There were all kinds of strange animals. They were wild animals, predators, killing machines, survivors, intent on hurting you or scaring you for life. There were all kinds of insects and snakes that could kill you just by touching you.

The Mposi people had made it seem so frightening because it was true.

They were only five Mposi residents who controlled 100 young people between 14 and 17 years of age. Above all of them, there was one whose words were like those of God.

Colonel de Mposi.

I hope little by little you are going to learn about him and who these residents are.

From this moment, my 40-year sentence began.

I was only 16 years old.

Chapter 13

Finally, we reached our destiny.

Mposi!

It was not a city. You could not call it a town or community either.

It was just a series of barracks. Five of them. They housed exactly 20 people aged between 12 and 17. They were brought here from anywhere on the continent. They were rich kids. During my first six weeks, I realized that their papas and mammies were as powerful as my father was. They ranged from petty thieves to murderers. The barracks were numbered MPOSI BARRACK 1, 2, 3, and so on. They called them simply M1, M2, M3, etc.

The barracks were large, with many windows but only two doors. The residents did not have a bed, bath or toilets. They slept on hammocks hanging from strong columns with iron hooks. They bathed outside under homemade channels of water coming down from a gigantic tanker above their head. If you did not prefer to do so, you were welcome to bathe in the river several miles from the campus. Three months from now, this tank would need to be filled up by the same residents who used it. Toilets were holes in the ground. Once they became full, they would close, and they would open another hole in the ground.

There was one kitchen and a dinner table for overseers and the man himself. Therefore, the barracks residents would allow them to find their own food and cook it on charcoal grounds beside the barracks, but if a barrack resident was caught stealing someone else's food, punishment would be severe.

These were the rules of Mposi.

There was the first rule.

Chapter 14

I arrived at night. There were torches here and there. I could not see anyone except a man who was walking towards us. He paid attention to the traveling officers next to me.

For the first time, I heard one of the Brazilian police officers' names. Carmelo Novoa. It would be the last time I would see him. Joe Mendoza, his partner, I would see several months later.

Novoa removed my handcuffs and said, "You must learn the game quickly. Otherwise you will die here, sonny boy."

I did not get what he meant right away, but, several weeks later, I did.

He turned and faced this Amazonian man against the dim light of the torches. It was impossible for me to get a clear look at him, but you have to believe me, I would have plenty of time to see his cocked face, froggy eyes, horse jaw, and that magnificent attitude that had, for the past thirty years, scared the hell of these kids. After a brief conversation, he and his partner strolled across the flat terrain and moved in the opposite direction. That was a mystery to me. I would learn that that side was a terrain of holes and abysses. How would these two get back to the civilized world? I would learn that mysterious secret not because they told me but because I found it out when I began figuring out how to escape from this place and accidentally noticed this was the only path to freedom.

Was my life linked to it?

"Hey boy! Get food on that table and you can stay wherever you like until tomorrow."

That was all.

I stood there not knowing what to do or where to go.

Chapter 15

Everything was strange to me. I had been spoiled since I had been inside Mom's belly. Mom did it. Dad did it as well. I commanded people to obey me. I did not have any shame in admitting it. I dictated. I had servants and chauffeurs, and I liked being in control of what I had. They worked for me. All of them worked for me. There was no question about it. I was a rich boy. I was a powerful young man. At this moment, I was lost in this world of darkness. It had started when I saw Verdis on the floor of my yacht. I sat back. I breathed. I could see only darkness. In reality, I would have months to comprehend the truth about where I was. Then, it hurt me and tears emerged from my fearful eyes.

I had to learn if I wanted to survive in this place.

What was strange was that, in this facility holding these 100 kids, there was no prison with wire bars or isolated rooms or solitary compartments. It was not a fortress, nor would I call it a mansion with British gardens and Italian courts. There were no watchtowers with men carrying long rifles and walkie-talkies with their big eyes behind sunglasses. No fences. No dogs. No patrolmen watching you through telescopes.

The place had a million acres of pure sugarcane plants. These sugarcane plants were tall like palm trees and they were part of the hard labor sentence that the Caribbean judge had imposed upon me. Would it be an easy sentence? I learned the hard way that it would not. There were also cafetal fields and woodlands that were part of my long sentence. Each kid here had to perform unquestioningly any task these five overseers commanded them to.

Escape?

You'd best think twice.

You'd have to know where you were going, and you'd have to know this place like a typical Brazilian indigenous person did. Otherwise, you would lose yourself in the forest, not knowing where to find a safe trail and be protected from the wild animals and poisonous snakes. If you survived the sucker mosquitoes, you would not survive the invisible creatures, the tinier killing insects or the slippery big cats.

If my description of this place seems exaggerated, you ought to consider it a jungle within another jungle, full of poisonous snakes, aggressive monkeys and black spiders.

It was clearly stated that there was no school and no counselor, but there were ten rules that appeared to confirm that you needed a backbone to survive in these sugarcane fields. Little by little, I will share these rules with you.

First rule:

Don't sleep on your own ignorance.

Chapter 16

After the evening bowl of rice and saucy pork, the introduction to the Authority was very simple.

"Welcome to Mposi," Rudolph Guerra said drily, smoking an undying homemade cigar. During my stay in this place, I did not see him without it between his sunbaked lips.

Everything about this individual was dry. His face, which was indeed cocked up by bites from God knows what, was made up of bones and scorched muscles. His jaw had been cut off by angry creatures. His brown eyes, with long eyebrows that almost buried them, stared viciously at his listener, making them feel chills of fear or repulsion. He dressed in black, an elongated Phantom jacket, a black Panamanian hat, heavy black boots, and it didn't matter if it was hot or cold, his attire never changed. The kids called him "the Black Shadow Ru" or addressed him with reference to his position in Mposi—Master Chief. If that name encapsulated Rudolph Guerra's personality, then you had a man as enigmatic as the place.

He was one of the overseers in Mposi and Master Chief of Barrack Number One, which he oversaw with iron fists, as the others were doing with theirs. There was a decision among them about who was going to take me. After they bet for my life as if I were a precious metal, I would be under the leadership of Mr. Guerra.

"You follow the rules and you will be alright."

He never told me what those rules might be, but I learned them the hard way.

Alejandro Sánchez, who introduced himself as the horse you cannot play with, brought with him a package, containing a single pair of pants, a single pair of boxer shorts, a single toothbrush and a single bar of soap, and he tossed all of them to me.

He looked at me carefully.

"You're a very handsome shiny boy," he observed. "If I were you, I would do something about that face."

I felt uncomfortable about such remarks. That would not be the last of them. I looked at Rudolph Guerra, who did not say a word, busy as he was selecting a pair of gloves and a machete from a dozen of them, all used and torn in part, except the machete. It was sharpened, just large enough to make sure your fingers were safe and the handler would remain firmly in your hands.

"You will be taught how to use the machete. It will take only five days for you to master it. After that, you will be recording 3,000 cane pounds per day. If you are below that, you will be in the field long enough to accomplish it."

"I've never done that."

I did not know how this man reached me, hit me with his open hand, and sent me flying several feet away

"Don't speak unless I ask you to do so."

I trembled with anger. How dare he! I was a Rockefeller! I got to my feet and moved towards him. I received the machete flat on my back. It hurt. I was angry. I felt nothing except my frustration. My father's absence and all that had happened during these months exploded in front of me. Any time I got close to him, I found myself on the ground, over and over. I was ready to jump forward, but I felt his shining boot on my chest. He pressed my chest hard.

"You will pay for this!"

"Before that I will crush you like a rabbit, daddy's boy!"

I struggled again. But he pressed his dirty boot down on my chest. Then it came. Human instinct. At this moment, I accepted my defeat.

He smiled.

"Four o'clock is the call to get up. You will supply your own breakfast, lunch and dinner. You will have a five-day break period until you learn to handle the machete, learn how to find food and how to preserve it like everyone in Mposi. You can find food anywhere, including here or there, but if we or they catch you stealing, you will restore what you have stolen, a month in the jungle, but you will still work in the field for your quota. Any questions?"

For the first time, I felt my pain overtaking my arrogance and pushing me to learn the game quickly enough to stay ahead of them. Otherwise, I would die in this jungle.

"Follow me!"

Chapter 17

Most of the kids were fully asleep. There was no privacy in this sleeping barrack. There were human smells and sounds of snores and of dreams of being hunted by sugarcane or running towards the woods. Several hammocks to my right was hook #5. I read what it said: *Ifo Comeaux. I was here. I will die here. God bless all of you.*

"This is your luxury suite room. Be sure to put your name on the slot."

I waited for him to tell me how to stretch out the hammock that was wrapped around the hook in the wall. He did not. He said finally, "Get some sleep. Four o'clock will be the call. Training starts right after that."

He turned and exited.

I stood there with my anger and pain. None of these kids made an effort to greet me or tell me how to fix the hammock.

Except one, and I heard him saying, "You must tighten up the end ropes to the hooky pole in good grips, and don't use that blank. It fills with leeches. And you should get as soon as possible a net for the sucker mosquitoes."

"Thanks."

"Don't bother, man. Make it work and get sleep. You will need it."

I tried to see his face. He was buried under his net.

A moment later, after I'd done all he'd told me to, I fell to the floor. I had not tightened it strongly enough, but I was too tired to do it again.

Chapter 18

Striking but galloping sounds reached me in paradise with a full English breakfast of back bacon, eggs, sausages, baked beans, bubble and squeak, fried tomatoes, fried mushrooms, black pudding with fried and toasted bread on the side and a glass of orange juice—all handed to me by my servant Harold Grogan on a silvery tray with *The Wall Street* morning newspaper. Good morning, Junior. Oh, morning. Mr. Grogan. Your breakfast, sir. Did my father leave the money I asked him to? Yes. He did.

There was a husky voice.

Then I felt a kick in my right side. Damn it! Pain reached my brain once more and I saw myself flying over the hammocks as I was hurled before the 20 kids already lined up on the dry terrain. At the same time, my pair of gloves and my machete were tossed in front of me. I continued to sleep as a strong arm grasped me by my neck and made me get up and line up with the others.

"Mornin' count."

"Say your name aloud. Start from you, Aram Agdain."

"Aram Agdain is here, sir!"

He whispered to me.

"Say your fucking name, man. You are going to make us work extra hours."

"William Rockefeller."

"And?"

"William Rockefeller, Junior."

"I don't care about your name, Mr. Shining Boy!"

"Say 'sir,' idiot," I heard from somewhere.

"William Rockefeller, sir!"

"Gilbert Ramirez, Master Chief!"

"Abdiel Butcher, sir!"

One by one, they said their names aloud until the kids' names had been recorded in the Guerra Log.

Barrack Number Two was across from us, not facing us but angled. Barrack Number Three was on the opposite side, creating a designed space in the center of the plaza, where Barrack Number Four occupied the left wing and made its kids unable to look at us or the others. Barrack Number Five was located up ahead to the right.

I could not tell whether these kids belonged to Barrack Number One. I was sure the kid who had helped me was Aram Agdain. I recognized him by his voice. A week later I would have a chat with him and learn why he was there. He insisted I called him Ares. I noted that all the kids had a surname. Also, most of the M1 residents had already eaten their breakfast and some had kept it for later. I had a question. How did they call us for breakfast?

No!

Mposi did not provide breakfast.

You did not have the right to luxuries like morning meals.

I learned this a week later, when my sugarcane cutting training ended and I asked Mr. Guerra for breakfast, and he told he had already explained the situation to me.

He laughed and sent me back to the line. He warned me that if I asked him again, he would cut my face. I didn't know whether he would, but I decided not to take such a risk.

Chapter 19

The training in handling the machete for the purpose of cutting sugarcane in the field was tough. It was a task I was to master in five days, and that was strenuous and punishing.

First, you needed to handle the long blade carefully, so as not to cut yourself. During those five days I cut myself 14 times: my legs, arms, fingers, and right side. Luckily, these wounds were not serious enough to send me to the Indian doctor several miles from Mposi field. Many residents who had inflicted on themselves such cuts did not make it.

Second, you had to hold the handle of the machete firmly, gripping it with your fingers and hand, sweeping with your arm in such a way that the machete would be far away from your belly and legs. Bending forward with your back in that position was a killer.

When I had completed my training, I could see the cut had not been perfect and the sugarcane root ended up looking like a mess.

At the same time, you had to turn the long sugarcane root to cut off its leaves, a technique you had to master. Otherwise, your hand would go with the cane.

Mr. Guerra was patient. He helped the first and the second time, but the third time he just watched me. I knew I was on my own. I could not master the sweeping of the arm, the skillful movement of my bent legs while at the same time keeping my back low.

It was all painful.

Ares could not help me with this one. By the time he reached the camp, he needed to cook or to find food for breakfast or lunch. He promised me the only way to master it was on the field.

In the field, I began getting to know the other kids. It surprised me that all of them were rich kids. With powerful papas. With powerful mamas. Even though they held titles as the only shareholders of several entities, they had been buried in these jungle barracks.

Criminals?

Oh yes.

It is going to shock you.

Chapter 20

Free breakfast had come to an end.

I noted that all the kids were cooking their own breakfast behind the Barrack Field, over charcoal or an oven made with wood from the forest. They had their spots, and they knew how it went. They were cooking rabbits, snakes, birds, frogs, and along with it they baked potatoes, plantain, roots or anything that came from the ground. Some of them made wraps with banana leaves and put them away in their improvised snakeskin bags.

Shaking my head, I walked to the main house to get my breakfast of wild eggs, bacon, bread and creamy goat milk.

"Hey, Rocke! Hey!" I felt someone grasp my arm and pull me aside. "Hey! What the hell are you doing?"

"I can ask you the same thing. Besides, my name is William Rockefeller, not Rocke."

"Hey! Relax. Everyone here has a nickname."

"You must be the one who sleeps next to me."

"Yeah."

He told me his name.

His name was Aram Agdain. They called him Ares. It was a habit among them. Everyone in my barrack had a nickname. I did not hear any of them tell me their real name. When I started to become familiar with the Mposi kids, I realized that they were to be recognized by their nicknames.

Ares was slender. He had small hazel eyes. His face was cocked with mosquito bites, a teen beard and dirty hair cemented against his skull. He was of medium build and behind the layer of dirt, I noted, he was a handsome 15-year-old young man. His father was Max Agdain, the one who founded the Dain Telephone Retain Company and had reported an annual revenue of 9.3 billion last year when he had made a deal with the Canadian Asses Firm.

"May I ask you a question?"

"What kind of question, man?"

"Hey, Rocke! I am not your enemy here, I tell you."

"I came here to get my breakfast."

"Are you kiddin'?"

"No. I am not kidding you."

"Say it again!"

There was the sound of a bell. Every kid ran to the main center of the plaza to line up in front of the blue flag. I saw that the flag only had a line of colors in green and blue. So I backed up and kept walking to the main house. I felt something hit me on my back, and then I heard the husky voice of Mr. Guerra.

"You, baby face," he said. "You're going in the wrong direction."

"I am trying to get my breakfast, sir."

"Your training ended yesterday, so the privileged breakfast, dinner, lunch and supper have gone. It's time to start your punishment. Cha-ca! Get in the line and into your position."

"But sir! I haven't eaten anything."

"You're going to figure it out tomorrow."

"That's bullshit!"

"Shut up, Rocke. Get in the line," Ares whispered, staring ahead, still, talking without looking at me.

"Get in line, Mr. Rockefeller," Mr. Guerra hissed.

"Tell this fool he will make us pay for his foolishness."

The speaker was Gilbert Ramirez. Gil. He was behind Ares. The kids of the barrack were nervous. Any interruptions during the group formation or in the sugarcane field and every one of us would face serious circumstances.

That was the rule. Unfair or not, there it was.

"You tried to be a hero," Solito Kuo said, looking at me as I started to back up. "You fool!"

"He is coming!"

"Oh shit!"

I wanted to talk more. A silence came upon us. Rudolph Guerra halted.

Colonel de Mposi appeared at the top of the slope. He ran his eyes over us. Then, with gigantic steps, he reached me. He raised his hand and smacked my face, sending me to the dry ground.

"I am Colonel de Mposi. Go!"

All the kids fell silent and looked at the ground.

Another humiliation.

But I learned this later.

I had to learn quickly, while I still had life in my veins.

Chapter 21

He was tall. Taller than my father was. Pure white skin. I did not know how he kept it out of the sun. His attitude was serene. Not like a military commander but like a black angel. Dressed like a Victorian British dandy in blue. A white handkerchief and tiny sunglasses made him look like a perfect professor of literature from the doomed Roman Academy. He called himself Colonel Ruth Canon de Mposi and his overseers the Black Knights of Mposi.

If I stayed, I would die. But I did not hold on to the sentiment that Mr. Mposi or his overseers were angels. I did not want to get ahead of what I was seeing and feeling. There was something that made me want to be careful and learn the ropes fast enough to beat the odds. As I have said previously, if I did not learn the rules or how to adopt, I would not make it.

I found myself on the floor, bleeding.

I had confidence that I could win against him. I was young. I was a Rockefeller. I looked at him. He appeared much older than he actually was, perhaps because the clothes he was wearing were gray, perhaps because he resembled my father.

Again!

I found myself on the wet ground.

I heard voices.

"Don't get up, you fool!"

"Don't fight!"

"You aren't goin' to win!"

He was there. He was untouchable.

I made another effort.

Although his expression was unchanging, his blue eyes were alert and that was when I thought I had had enough.

Chapter 22

I opened my eyes to the blue sky above me. Sounds and voices came towards me in layers.

Like an unfortunate worm ready to be devoured by an eagle, I sat on the ground covered in sugarcane roots, my machete and my pair of gloves next to me.

Rudolph Guerra's face appeared before me.

"Welcome back. You'll couple yourself up with Aram. Get movin', boy."

I tried to speak. I couldn't. He smirked at me. There was no pity. There was no word that would alleviate the agony around my jaw. At that moment, he looked at me as if I were a belligerent bulldog dropped in an unknown world. After all the physical punishment Colonel de Mposi had given me, Mr. Guerra's smirk disappeared and finally I heard some comments from him, and I heard myself reply that no one was going to break me.

I was wrong.

Chapter 23

"You are a fool. Do you think you are the only one who hates this place?"

I looked at Ares several feet from me, cutting sugarcanes with elegance, using his brawny right arm and sending them back with speed to the same spot behind him. I was so upset that I could not focus on forming words. I could not think straight about what would come next. What I knew was that I could not stand it there any longer.

"Cut the cane, Rocko! Jesus! They're going to force us to work extra hours if we do not complete our quota." Tony Popovic or Popo made some signals I could not follow.

We were a team of six. We moved across the sugarcane field. I was unable to figure out how to cut sugarcane and deal with the dilemmas I faced at Mposi. Our team consisted of Aram "Ares" Agdain, Gilbert "Gil" Ramirez, Solito "Sot" Kuo, Abdiel "But or Ab" Butcher, Kank "Al" Aldridge and me. While I was still pissed off about being called "Rocko," I was not as good at cutting sugar as they were. Close to us was the rest of the M1 team. I recognized their leader was a boy named Greg "Big" Cruz whom I did not like. I did not know who the leader of our group was. I presumed it was Ares.

What I did notice, however, was that we had the same responsibility as a group and when the time arrived, we shared the same quota during the time we were in the field.

"Why is Rocko standing there instead of cutting sugarcanes?" Ab said.

"Shut up, Ab, right? Shutta fuck up!" I said.

"You want to be tough with me, Rocko?" Ab said.

"Cut it out, you two!" Gil whispered between his teeth. "Mr. Guerra is watching us!"

"I'll leave this place. You guys will see."

They laughed.

"You'll learn, Rocko."

"I've told you, don't call me that. I'm William Rockefeller or William or Will, understand?"

"Oh, you are a little snot and wrapped up in the grace of snobbishness!"

Three boys were carrying sugarcane across the field. Ares made gestures to them that made me presume they were deaf or something. It turned out there was a language the kids in Mposi had created and used to communicate amongst themselves. It was so effective that they could communicate long-distance without any problem at all.

The message was simple.

The gestures had said, "Eyes, Inn and Ta. Hey boys, meet Rocko. He's the newest member of our sugarcane team. Say hi to him."

They glanced at me and, through movements of their hands, they replied.

"Hello, Rocko."

"Be alert. Or you die."

"Welcome to paradise, sweetie."

I looked at Ares. I tried to speak, but he gestured in a different direction. In the distance, Mr. Guerra was making his way to us. He came to me and saw that I had not done anything. He looked at Ares, which seemed to confirm that he was the leader of the team. He did not speak. He backed off.

"What did you say to them?"

"Nothin'."

"Are they mute or deaf?"

"No. It's our language. You'll learn it."

"Don't need it. Soon, I'll be gone."

"I want to tell you something, and you must listen to me good, Rocko."

"You can come with me, man. One phone call and they will come to get me."

"Oh, you will not understand."

He kept cutting sugarcane roots.

Eyes. Inn. Ta. They tossed sugarcane roots into the pile. They moved back. They made gestures with their hands.

Remember! It was the Mposi language.

Eyes said, "Where do you come from?"

Paulo "Eyes" Hayes, 15, skinnier than an earthworm, was the son of Chief Justice Bar Hayes in Michigan. He had embarrassed his dad by stealing a pencil from Connie Market and giving it to his girlfriend, Nancy Fajeston, the only daughter of Benjamin and Rachel Jenkings, owners of Remy, Jacoste & Emiling International Insurance, which had a presence in Middle Eastern, Asian, and Australian territories. She had denied any involvement by telling her father she didn't know how that pencil had got into her backpack.

"New York."

"Vancouver. Canada."

"Why so far away?"

"Dad. He told me I needed to experience pain."

Eyes said, "You have to know how to cut sugarcane."

"Not for me."

"I had that attitude before I reached this place, and now it's changed."

"Not for me, I tell you."

"It will be."

Chapter 24

I am running through the sugarcane fields. I keep running. I run to the right. I run to the left. I want to turn. Right or left? Right! I make a right turn. I make a left turn. I am running away from this place. Not daring to look back for fear that someone is after me. I run along the narrow avenue on which wagons are carrying the sugarcane plants somewhere. I follow the narrow avenue. I jump over a dead animal. I think that's what it is. I keep moving. I know that with this speed I will eventually find the main road.

I crash against sugarcane pants. I fall. I get up. I walk. I jog. Then I begin to run, fast. My eyes hurt because of the sugarcane leaves that slap my face. My arms and feet start to bother me, but I do not stop running.

I halt. I take a deep breath.

I look right. I look left. I look ahead of me. What I see is the sugarcane, sugarcane, and sugarcane everywhere.

Where, William? Think. Think. Think.

I am thinking. In front of me is the green curtain of the sugarcane fields, and I hear the birds somewhere. Strange creatures are watching me, and snakes, and those invisible spectators and ghosts who are telling me what my next move should be. I feel at a loss, as I do not know where to go.

I need to do something. So, I start running once again. A moment or two later, I lose track of where I am going. So much sugarcane. Too many parallel sugarcane fields and infinite lines of green ghosts.

I see only sugarcane, not a forest, not a countryside road, not a car, but sugarcane fields. Fully recognizing that my very life is hanging in the balance here in this green world, I begin to feel all the necessities. I feel thirty. I feel my belly and I feel I must go to a place where I will find water, food and a way to get out of these damned fields of sugarcane.

Think, Wiliam, think! Where is north? Where is south? Think, man. You are a Harvard student. You are smart. Use your knowledge. Remember Columbus. Marco Polo. Do it.

I turn around, and I start using my hands to find north and south.

I think I have got it. I set off on a trail of sugarcane.

Yes, yes, yes.

Forest. Trees. Wind of freedom. I smell cooking.

It is just an illusion. I am right back where I started. I emerge behind the Mposi encampment. It cannot be.

No!

It cannot be.

It is impossible.

But it is true.

Chapter 25

The five ghosts were standing along the edge of the encampment. It seemed they were not waiting for me, but they were. They sniggered at me. They seemed so powerful, so invincible.

Rudolph Guerra glanced at me. I was in pain. It is impossible for me to describe myself, but I was bleeding, my feet were swelling, my face was itching and my body was on fire. There were all kinds of insect bites all over my body.

"Mr. de Mposi wants to see you."

I did not know what time it was. I did not know how many miles I had been running in circles. I had been moving around in the same spot. This was when the kids returned from the fields. Many of them had finished cooking and bathing and had gone to sleep.

I saw some kids standing in front of the M1 barracks. Ares appeared below the ravine, carrying a couple of rabbits across his shoulders. He halted to have a look at me, but he did not say a word because of Mr. Guerra's presence. He shook his head with disappointment.

A moment later, I was in the presence of Colonel de Mposi.

He sat behind a gigantic table filled with ribs, corn, fried plantain, rice, bread, fruits and a bottle of wine. It was his dinner time, and a native woman whose name I did not catch was serving him. It was the first time I had seen her, but it was not the last.

She was serving him rice. She was dressed nicely but not in that celebrity style I had become accustomed to seeing in Paris, New York, England or Italy.

He wore a white kimono. It made him look like a distinguished Kamakura shogun in this jungle deep in Brazil. His long gray hair waved sensuously around his perfect skull. He smelled good. Everything about this man was as mysterious as it was fascinating.

"Sit."

I looked at him. Then I peered down at the food. Suddenly, the smell of food made me remember that I had not eaten anything since the previous day.

"What is your full name, boy?"

"Excuse me?"

"Don't question me!"

"I don't understand you."

"What is your full name, I ask you?"

"William Rockefeller."

"You live in Mposi, do you not?"

"No. I live in New York!"

"That was before the accident in the Bahamas."

"How dare you, sir!"

"Be careful. Again, where do you live?"

"I have been telling you."

"Where do you lay down, sonny boy?"

I looked at the native woman, but she did not have any interest in what was going on. She was only interested in feeding this Victorian aristocratic master. Mr. Guerra was silent against the wall.

I took a deep breath. "Temporarily, I am lying here."

De Mposi made a notation on a log that was next to him. He picked up a rib with a golden folk, and he held it before him.

"How long have you been living here?"

I tried to make sense of his ridiculous interrogation. I wanted to make sense of it. It was very important to know where he wanted to go with these questions.

"Forty-five days."

"I see you have a problem addressing people who are more important than you. You don't address those above you as sir, madame, colonel, and I can see now you are still a wild tiger, but I know a year from now your second personality is going to tell you that you need to change that silly arrogance of yours. So, what is your occupation here?"

I thought of saying "student" or nothing, but those would not be the right replies.

"A sugarcane cutter."

He took the rib to his mouth. He chewed slowly, wiped his lips with an elaborate white cloth, and then drained half a glass of wine. I could see he enjoyed these psychological games. I wondered if he had read Freud, Skinner, Watson or one of my favorites, Jung.

"Is your behavior acceptable?"

"No, sir."

"Should the other kids be punished because of your behavior?"

"No, sir."

"What kind of punishment do you think we will impose on you?"

"I need to speak with my father."

Patiently, he started over again.

"What is your full name, boy?"

He repeated all of this ten times, until I correctly answered the question about the punishment for my behavior.

He glanced at Rudolph.

"You heard it, Señor Guerra. Send him back to the field and let him complete his quota."

"You cannot send me again to the field."

"I can do whatever I please with you, Mr. William Rockefeller. I am God here, and you will learn that one way or another."

"I do not know how to cut the sugarcane."

"Well, we gave you five days to master the cutting, and your stupidity has blown it. You must master it, Mr. Rockefeller. You must."

Chapter 26

I was unable to see any longer where the sugarcane I was cutting or snapping with the machete was. This was not a problem. They made me see. They brought me an *antorchas*. They looked at me working. They played judge and jury. They both took brutal pleasure in seeing a teenager break down in tears. This place would not hold me. I knew for a fact that I would escape again.

After hours of cutting sugarcane and carrying it to the trail, I could not feel my arm and I could not feel the machete.

The machete had become heavier. My hands burned because the gloves I had been given had torn, exposing the delicate skin of my hands to the hard handle of the machete. This made me slow down. It made me curse everyone, including my dad.

They told me to stop.

Mr. Guerra examined the sugarcane I was supposed to cut like a professional. The cuts were bad. He saw I was leaving pieces of pure sugarcane attached to the roots. He ordered me to do it again. I faced him with the machete at my left side. Mr. Guerra was calm. He was like a pharaoh.

"I can't."

"Look! He's going to cry," Josh Hansel said mockingly. "Let me take your tears."

"Josh!"

"But just look at him."

I gazed at Josh and then I gazed back at Mr. Guerra. I backed up. They wouldn't make me out to be a sissy, and Josh Hansel had made me grow.

I did what Mr. Guerra instructed me to do.

I cut the remaining roots of the sugarcane.

He ordered me to pick up the sugarcane and carry it to the edge of the road for tomorrow's pick-up.

Hours later, when the owl was calling at the moon, I heard him say, "You're done."

Mr. Guerra, Dieng Chung, Miguel Bojorques and Ranjit Sandhu followed him. Josh Hansel remained dumbfounded.

"If you ask for help among the kids of Barrack Number Three, you are not going to work as hard as you did today. If you refuse, well, I will take care of that for you, sweetie."

It was one of the mysterious insinuations that came constantly from this man. I was too tired to figure out his dark intentions. I needed a couple of months to understand what his words meant. I learned from the other kids that I needed to be wary of him. His intentions were not good and I had to play safe in front of him. I began to see this was not a picnic but an entanglement. You had to be strong to survive; otherwise, the bigger fish would track you to dangerous corners and you would not make it.

There were rules I was not yet familiar with.

With shooting pains in my back, my hands burning, and my stomach filled with gas, I lay in the hammock. My body was aching. My hands had swelled and my mind was empty.

"Hey, Rocko!" Etmo "Witz" Markowitz of Barrack Number Three was across the narrow corridor, if one would call it that. He wore shorts and carried a tin cup and bread. "I know you are not eating anything. I got something for you."

I looked at him. He smiled innocently. I didn't see anything wrong in his eyes. He was a young man of medium height. I presumed he was 16 or 17. You could not tell because of his long and dirty face. He was a kind of well-built young man, a strong kid, a player, with a reputation for being a bully. At this moment, he was a sweetheart ready to help.

"Thanks."

I took the tin cup and the bread, which was stuffed with meat and wild tomatoes. I knew the kids were watching. I did not know if Ares was sleeping or not. By the time I took a bite of the bread, Witz' hand had reached my leg.

"What the hell are you doing, Witz?"

"I need a favor from you, that's all."

"Hey!"

At this moment, Ares made his appearance from the windows. He carried a bag attached to his chest, and he watched us while others were getting out of their hammocks. I heard the kids talking.

"What is going on?"

"Witz."

"Hey!"

"It's a favor."

"You fool."

"You take the cup and your bread. Fuck off!"

"It's too late. I will collect that beautiful gift from you. You are all mine!"

I stepped out of the hammock. He did not expect me to face him. He grasped my penis and squeezed it. "Goodness! You're hungry already."

I was still a Rockefeller but before Witz I was just a sissy.

Again, he did not expect my reaction.

He backed up, but I was ready. With my hands on fire, I faced him. I made all my movements count. This was not like a fight in a teen club or what had happened on the yacht. It was indeed a teen fight for reputation and morals. It was a fight to send a message to all the kids in Mposi that I was not going to take any shit from anyone.

"They are coming!"

The overseers were there, including Mr. Guerra and Mr. Hansel.

"What is happening here?"

As I was about to explain the situation, Ares stood in front of me and faced Mr. Guerra. "Nothing, General Chief, Witz has come here to ask Rocko how he was feeling. He took it the wrong way, you know how it goes."

Mr. Hansel was furious, as he saw Witz bleeding. Later, I knew he was responsible for sending Witz to me.

Mr. Guerra was cool. "Truth, Mr. Rockefeller?"

"Truth, General Chief."

He looked over at Witz. "Mr. Markowitz?"

"Yes, sir. It's the truth."

"Take your boy, Mr, Hansel."

He commanded it with a brutal gesture. He tossed a hand around Witz' neck and pulled him out of the barrack.

"Well. Show is over. Ladies, go back to sleep!"

I moved to the hammock, and I stood there. I examined mentally whether I had been hit or touched by Witz. No.

Ares and Gil came to me. Ares handed me several pieces of rabbit. Gil was holding the tin cup and the bread.

"You deserve it. You won."

"Don't want it."

"Eat! It was a clear fight, and you got him," Ares explained.

Gil glared at me. "Tomorrow your name will be on people's lips. You are a warrior of Mposi. You hit Witz. There will be another challenger."

"He isn't going to take it lightly. Besides, he has back-up from the sick bastard Josh."

"I will keep breaking him."

"You need to play safe. He has a handful of bees behind him."

Gil paused. "You need to learn our rules, how to hunt and to keep food, Rocko."

"This isn't my permanent house."

"It is now. We will teach you to communicate, steal food, hunt and be smarter in the field after you decide to do what you feel is right. Remember, each one of us is trying to escape. I have done it 11 times, and they have always caught me and brought me back. So I made the decision to do it in an intelligent way or I will die here."

"I know. I've tried. Fourteen times," Ares said.

I heard one by one their stories of escape, and I was thinking about Devil's Island, where Henri "Papillon" Charrière made his final escape.

"Otherwise, you go to eat, and keep these fried rabbits safe, and try to find a net. Six months from now, your body will be covered in mosquito bites. That isn't good."

"How can I find a net?"

"Number one: be smart."

<h1 style="text-align:center">Chapter 27</h1>

In the morning, I could hold nothing with my hands.

Kank "Al" Aldridge, a member of the Ares group, said, "Pee on your hands."

"What?"

Ares and Gil were preparing their breakfast and boiling up the water for coffee. Gil turned and looked at me.

"Yes, Rocko! It can alleviate the pain until your hands are cured."

But Jet made another suggestion: to wrap my hands with mud and black roots from the low canyon site, a place I had never heard of before. Others suggested that I should use horse shit. I kept hearing more suggestions and when I followed each of them, the blisters in the palms of my hands started popping and exploding.

We had time to talk more and socialize amongst ourselves until Gil began to teach me the rules of communication. It was hard at first. Making the "m," "p," "k" "z," "x" and "ph" gestures was complicated but, day by day, I worked on mastering the first rule and they made me observe how they did it.

Ares and Gill would communicate with their hands, and Sot and But would ask me what they were saying.

Solito "Sot" Kuo was a privileged son and the most manic among us. He was born Michael Popovec Solito Kou of Choy, a mix of Chinese, Cambodian, and Islander. His daddy was Mr. Aram Kou, married to his Hong Kong high school sweetheart in London, who gave him only one child. She died when he was only seven and, believe it or not, it had affected the little young Kou since. Unlike my own story, his father sent him to the best schools in China, Hong Kong, Spain, Germany and Turkey. Sol started to use drugs and hang out with the Boz Three gang in Chicago. Not taking any chances, Mr. Kou sent him to a special school in Scotland. He grew fast, learning about sex, using pistols and spending money like a little crazy gangster. It was then that the criminal record of his son made Mr. Kou act. He hit someone (an important person, as Sol put it), costing the old man more than $100 million to settle it outside the British Royal Court.

"That judge took only a minute to give me 17 years, man, and that made me think, how did Pop let this happen? He is a very, very rich man. I am the only son. Can you decode that?"

He was his only son and he was going to receive $100 billion plus when his dad decided to retire. Whatever his pop (and mine) was thinking, it was unfair of him to think the only way to control his son or to make him understand reality was to send him to a place like this. Perhaps Sot and I would start to see the other aspect of our existence and the gigantic effort our daddies were making to save us.

At this moment, we did not understand yet, as our stories had just started unfolding. We were unable to see the truth.

Gilbert Ramirez' father was a monopolist of communication and transportation in Mexico. Gil was a bad boy, and he was not the only one in his family. He had followed in his elder brother's footsteps. The latter was in a gang, even though none of them needed to be in one. James Ramirez was a member of the Vera Cruz Notary Gang. On July 10, James Ramirez was killed by a single bullet fired directly into his head. Gil could have been killed when he witnessed his brother dying in his arms. He was the one who was going to follow his dad into the business and lead the company, and when his brother died that day, his dad hoped that Gil would follow him, but the young Gil was out of control. He had lost his old man's trust, and Don Ramirez tried to make him understand. He sent an elite group to Hawaii, where Gil was living, and when Gil opened his eyes, he had to face this reality, and the rest was history.

He said, "I want revenge." He wanted to kill not only the Vera Cruz Family, but the entire world. "I see only shadows. I wouldn't listen to my mother, my father, or my youngest brother. They did all they could to hold me. But I was out of control."

"You burned the entire house?" I asked.

"Yes."

"The family? What happened to the family?"

"Rocko, let it rest."

"No, it's all right, Sol. We're here for some reason. We're ill-omened, I guess."

"Sorry, Gil."

"She was there. They did not make it in time to save her. I tried, you know. It was the nine-year-old Becky," said Gil, his eyes tearing up. "That was a mistake, I know."

There was a long silence.

Ares passed the cup filled with coffee. We drank coffee, and, as we chewed sugarcane with it, I considered Gil's case. His father, like mine, could save him, but had decided against it when he ran to their Honolulu getaway estate. Gil's father was as rich as my daddy.

It could be true that we were ill-omened, as Gil said, or that we did not have the ability to see the future. Our fathers and mothers were anxious to save us from the wrecked way we had chosen. I did not dare to voice my thoughts, but each story that I heard gave me that impression. I knew for a fact that money could buy everything—couldn't it? I was curious.

We looked at Ares, But and then Al. None of them was ready to open up before me. I guess it was up to me. To understand our choices as kids was not easy. Never would be. Still, I think in the case of each son, except for Jet and Eyes, who did not have dads, rather mums, I recognized there was a temptation or compulsion to be noticed by his daddy that I hoped to understand somehow.

There were a few minutes left until the final call to move to the sugarcane fields. Al and But were making every effort to teach me to use traps, knots and projectiles to hunt animals after it became clear that none of them wanted to go further and tell me more family stories and why they had ended up there.

It was then that Witz slipped into our territory. He was not alone. With him was a handful of kids with bad attitudes who were ready to rumble.

Everyone was tense.

He spoke. "I will break that pussy of yours."

"You trespass, Witz," said Ares, standing up. He was followed by Gil, Al and Sot.

"He's mine, I tell you." He backed up, and then moved away.

Gil looked at Ares. "He will not stop, Ares, you know that."

"This is my fight, you guys."

"No, Rocko. You do not understand," Sot said. "You're one of us. This is our fight as well."

"I'm not scared of him."

Ares wrapped up his lunch and water and coffee in bamboo. "Keep an eye out, Rocko. You've to learn how to communicate fast. Most importantly, these signs." He showed me a move.

"What was that?"

"'Be careful,'" Al said. "These two fingers left is B-E and palm up toward you is C-A-R-E-F-U-L. And elbow right is 'I will.'"

The call was made.

All the kids marched to the plaza with their respective teams or barracks.

"Let us hear Barrack One. Say your name aloud."

"Romeo Posada, sir!"

"Burt Holland, chief!

"Aram Agdaian, Master Chief!"

"William Rockefeller, Master Chief!"

When the 94 names were counted, the overseers gathered in the middle of the plaza. According to Ares' report, six kids were missing from Barrack Two. They were Christopher "C.D." Davis and DeVon "Vony" Curtin. From Barrack Three, Jason "Y" Yadiro had been missing since the previous week, and from Barrack Fourt, Ronald "Egg" Eng, James "Rock" Estavrook, and Bolaji "Fan" Fanti were missing.

There was a rumor. Josh Hansel had something to do with the disappearances, along with the culprit Witz. It was just a rumor, but it seemed those rumors fell heavily on Mr. Hansel's shoulders, when James and Ronald had been transferred from Barrack Three to Barrack Four. A moment later, Colonel de Mposi appeared.

Dieng Chung of Barrack Five, Miguel Bojorquez of Barrack Four, Josh Hansel of Barrack Three, Ranjit Sandhu of Barrack Two and Rudolph Guerra walked to Colonel de Mposi, and he had a conversation with them.

They handed him the morning log.

Colonel de Mposi looked at Mr. Sandhu and nodded. Mr. Sandhu stood in front of his team. Colonel de Mposi held a private chat with Josh. He talked. He listened to Josh Hansel, and then waved him back to his barracks.

He walked to the middle of the square.

"Good morning, Colonel de Mposi," everyone said at once.

"Good morning!" Then he made his speech, and after that he called Mr. Guerra. Both men looked in my direction.

An hour later, exactly when the owl called to the moon, we began to march to the sugarcane fields.

Chapter 28

I began to master the art of cutting. I was planning to escape after the first call, which would be roughly when the sun reached the center of the heavens. I began to see that the other part of the sugarcane field ought to offer another way of getting onto the right trail towards the small town.

The sun was not out but the heat was already intolerable.

You had to be careful about snakes, scorpions and sucker creatures that could send you to your deathbed if you did not arrive at the hospital on time. The local hospital was managed by a local Indian somewhere in the jungle.

Many of Barrack Number One's residents were ahead of me and there was no way I could reach them. I was the only one behind, but they understood I was doing my best under the circumstances to catch up.

The waterboy pulled up with a mule and called out. A few boys came to get water from him and I was one of them. I filled up two bamboos with water.

"They are talking about you everywhere."

I looked at Cara Roja, and he tried to avoid my glance.

"What did you say, Cara Roja?"

"I heard Witz is going to hit you, Rocko. Be careful, hear me?"

I wanted to know what he meant but he did not speak. A strange boy by the name of Mel "Eel" Elinghton approached us. He looked at me. He was a resident of M4. He filled up his elaborate bag made of dog skin and said, "Watch out! You'll be hunted like a butterfly."

"Where did you hear that?"

But Lagi, as many called him, backed up and moved away from us. I looked around as Col, Vill and Yu, led by Witz, strolled across the sugarcane field.

"You should be going, Rocko."

I did not defend myself against the name this time as I began to walk to my team. I was a little concerned. *Do I make my move and face them?* I would rather make my move to leave. There it was.

Chapter 29

At a fast pace, struggling over the sugarcane roots in the field, I made my escape.

I told myself to move north, no matter what the outcome. North would be a good direction to head in if I wanted to get out of this remarkable geography of sugarcane fields, which I had never seen so many of at such high density.

I had water and food and my feet were wrapped up nicely with rabbit's skin. I did not dare to remove my shirt, even though I was boiling in the heat. With the machete in my hands, I opened the way up.

I assured myself, in an offhand manner, that I did not mind pain. Trying to avoid these dangerous creatures could hurt me.

Deep in the fields of sugarcane I walked and was ready to make the second decision: whether to go a little south, then follow the sun to my left. I could still see only sugarcane fields, and a sense of panic rose inside me. I did not know if I was lost or this was a world of only sugarcane plants entirely and they had lied to us—we were not in any part of Brazil.

We were in hell, and it angered me that, in spite of all my efforts to be calm and focused, I was not prepared for the vast expanse of forest.

The sun was now behind me. I took a long, deep breath. I could not risk making another mistake. I was sure I was ahead of Mposi Campus. The sun just kept getting hotter. I was not sure what time it was. This could not fool me either. I was not sure it was noon.

I stopped. I could see more than five feet, and I entered a world of fear, anxiety and paranoia. I saw tall green men moving, laughing, mocking me and making me lose my sense of where I was.

A thought hit me.

I thought about quitting. I wondered what they would do to me. Force me to cut more sugarcane, hold me before the Colonel of Mposi, make me listen to his paternal speech about my behavior? What would happen to the others? The promise of being together as a team? It did not matter to me. They were not my family or people I was attached to.

Chapter 30

This escape had been a disaster since I left the campus.

According to my calculations, based on the several attempts I had made, going north would give me an advantage and allow me to see the landscapes, the forest routes, human presence or towns that were not related to Mposi. I hadn't seen anything of that sort, and I was certain this wasn't the right trail on which to exit the place.

I followed the birds, who gave me throughout much of my time on the walk a sense of orientation. But these birds were too far away for me to keep up with them. On two occasions, birds whose flights were too high made me lose my sense of time.

I had only one bamboo filled with water, and my food was gone, and each time I was prepared to make the final decision to go back I realized I was lost.

Now the sun was above me. Somehow, I appeared to see things and to know things that the others often missed. For instance, that all was not lost. If I kept up a straight line, I would end up at something, a ravine, a canyon, a group of Indians. No field could be so long or so wide. There had to be an end. It was only logical. Now a new hope had seized me. I continued ahead. My water was gone but I still had the juice of the sugarcane.

The direction of the sun changed.

I knew for a fact that east was an important direction and that the Earth rotates or spins towards the east, and that's why the sun, moon, planets and stars all rise in the east and make their way westwards across the sky. Every school student knows it, that, in short, the sun rises in the east and sets in the west because of our planet's rotation.

I observed the sun. It was above me. After a long walk, I was able to see nothing, and the sun was to my right. Again, I remembered. The sun rises exactly due east and sets exactly due west on only two days of every year. Sunrises and sunsets happen because the Earth spins counter-clockwise if we look down at the North Pole. The Earth's tilt means there are only two days per year that the sun rises exactly due east.

I stopped. I closed my eyes and concentrated, telling myself to relax, that everything would be all right, but *you need to concentrate, William.* I summoned up the knowledge I had gained from my teachers, Mrs. Smjr, Mrs. Gaaer and Mr. Acho.

Slowly, I opened my eyes and opened my arms, and I started searching the sky. I found it. I faced Polaris. I was facing north, so behind me was south, and west would be on the left and of course east would be on my right.

Having recalled this lecture of Mr. Acho, I breathed a little.

I looked left. I saw now I had been wrong all along.

I was not ready to quit, and with renewed hope, I ambled left.

You should have known this a long time ago, William.

Well, I got it, right?

Sure?

Yes. I am sure.

Remember, the sun... the Earth...

I am not stupid, man, okay? I know.

Cutting my way with the machete, I felt a new impulse had taken me. I felt nothing, neither thirst nor hunger.

The plants here had grown more than 20 meters tall, and their stout, joined, fibrous stalks made it impossible to break through.

I continued. Butterflies, moths, ants and termites were everywhere.

A sound.

I halted.

I looked up. The sun was setting.

I heard sounds at a distance again. I stood there. I peered through the plants in the field. I had seen no wild animals or any predators. As I grew confident, I saw the natural concentrations of many beauties around me. It appeared to touch me from everywhere. It appeared to elevate me over the landscapes and above the dimly lit sunset sky, from where I could see the prominent hills with their timber forests and red peaks with water racing through them and the depth of the canyon below. The pure earth's storehouse of a hundred insects. The sun-spark in the unknown stream and the fresh air. From somewhere came the sounds, voices, converted into far-reaching songs of ghosts. I heard the music.

I cried at this discovery. Nothing is eternal. A teen like me should have known that.

I had to be very careful because the First Law of Probability states that the results of one chance event have no effect on the results of subsequent chance events.

I heard sounds, voices. However, as what I heard indicated a human presence, I had to be careful and concentrate on the probability until the next task.

Danger.

It was important to realize that I was alone, having walked more than 100 kilometers between grasses and roots.

The Black Shadow watched the Barrack Number One residents gathering in the plaza for the evening count.

The kids were exhausted. Their faces were covered with dirt, bites and blood. But they were talking about the latest news.

Rocko.

The big-mouthed Rocko was missing. So were Torl from M2 and Basel from M3.

Everybody knew that Rocko had been gone since the cutting of the sugarcane roots in the morning. He had escaped.

The kids lined up around the plaza.

Ab came close to Ares. "Do we expect he got it?"

"Only the Forest Ghost will know that, Ab."

"What a fool!"

Al changed positions with Gil to get closer to Ares and Ab and Sol.

"Did you know what he was going to do?"

"He isn't a brother to me."

"He started to like you, Ares."

"What did he say, Ares?"

"Nothing," Ares replied. Then he glanced at Gil and Sol, saying, "It doesn't matter to me. An escape is another escape."

"He'll come back as it is," Popo observed.

"Ready. Let us hear your names," Mr. Guerra's voice rebounded in the plaza. "Say your names out loud."

"Kank Aldridge, Master Chief."

"Ares," Sol called.

"You're going to get us in trouble, Sol. What's the point?"

"Are you upset at what Rocko has done?"

"Not really, Sol. It's his call."

"We should start it again."

"Aram Agdain is here, Master Chief."

"Gilbert Ramirez is present, sir."

"Popo."

He peered at Ab.

"I say he couldn't care less about us. He could have told us. We trusted him."

"Don't blame him, Popo."

"No, Sol. No. I don't."

"William Rockefeller."

Silence.

"Absent."

Stepping out from among the massive sugarcane plants, I wandered aimlessly through the forest until I found myself walking by the edge of a dangerous gully. Carefully, I stepped on the edge of firm terrain and looked down into the black and deep hole. I couldn't understand how I had got here— no roads, no towns, and I was between two enormous hills and a distance of 100 kilometers from the other side of the unknown land.

I thought I might have found a bridge. Even if I did not reach a town, couldn't I see where the voice or sound had come from?

I backed up. Not moving to the sugarcane plants, but along the edge of the canyon.

All the sounds had stopped.

Now there was a place in the rainforest where the hills ran straight up, and they were so smooth that no one had ever climbed them, even though the bushlands, the edges, were part of this vast land. I had no forest experience.

It was not until the hills turned into a jungle that I began noting I was somewhere near a canyon.

The sun began to call it quits.

I was a little concerned about where to find food and a place to sleep, and I was not heading to the slopes. Then I suddenly remembered my promise to keep the big star before me.

I wasn't afraid about losing the star; rather, I was afraid of being swallowed by the darkness.

There it was.

Darkness took over.

Ares, Gil, Popo and Ab were talking about me and Witz.

"He decided to escape because he could not face Witz."

"Cut it out, Ab. You don't need to bring this subject up now. We're eatin'."

"You can't see the truth. They call him a coward, and that is going to hurt us, too."

Gil spoke. "You done warming those frogs, Ab?"

"I'm finishin'."

"What now, Ares?"

Ares said nothing as he bit into the grilled snake.

"I thought so."

"Rocko isn't a coward, Ab."

"Really, Gil?"

Ab walked to the group and considered Ares. He sat among the group. He started picking up frogs and tossing them in grill.

"We will die if we don't do something about it. We still have family, with money."

"We've done nothing since our last attempt to escape." Sol appeared, carrying a large vase filled with sugarcane juice. "All of us have ended up in the same spot."

Ares stretched his arm and grasped one of the sweet mushrooms. He didn't even look at them, especially not Sol. He ate quietly. They considered him.

"Ares."

"Yeah."

"Where is your mug?"

He looked down at his mug, took it, and handed it to Sol. He poured some sugarcane juice into it. "You heard the news. About Rocko's escape. He did it because he was scared to face Witz."

He took the mug from Sol, and he did not reply.

"He knows that, Sol."

"I heard. That's so."

Sol sat and served frogs, mushrooms and fried snakes. He began to eat. He paid attention to Popo.

"I cannot explain what is going on," Popo was saying. "I try telling those guys Rocko isn't a coward. He just doesn't want to be here. Was I such a bad boy?"

They kept their eyes on Popo.

But there was no comment and, under the ambiguous light of the torches on both sides, their faces looked like unfinished portraits.

What Sol was saying was true. First it was Al, Sol and Gil. They left Mposi after the evening counting, at night and with plenty of food, but six days later, the trio were exhausted, lying in a place called Chaparral. Almost dying. They were lucky that Ab and Ares found them. They, too, were lost, and during these four nights and four days each one was struggling for his life.

None of the overseers made any effort to look for them, but there they could do nothing else.

I stopped. My stomach was hurting. I was hungry, thirsty and exhausted. I couldn't move further. A killer headache was just what I didn't need. My body needed protein.

I started searching for food. I had seen Ares, Gil and Sol do it. I focused on trying to find something quickly and easily.

It would be difficult to catch a bird or snake and would take hours to build a trap or dig into these bushlands when I had no light. I decided to search for termites, but I changed my mind because I would need a large quantity and that would be time-consuming. So, I focused on worms, bees, wasp larvae and snails.

I had never done it before, even though they had insisted on me doing so.

I collected them. I got mealworms, grubs, sand wasp larvae. It always seemed to me that there was a first time for everything. After this, I could eat almost anything.

Returning to the sugarcane field, I took a couple of canes and, with the machete, cut them into cubes. I began to eat my delicious but gross mealworms, grubs and wasp larvae.

At first it was a struggle, and it struck me as a strange taste, but later it was just as tasty as a platter of lobster or shrimp.

By this time, I could not see a thing, and every sound of the earth had more impact on me than anything else.

I missed my bed, my room, the attention of my private servant. I missed being called Rockefeller Junior.

Then, the sounds of voices, far away, down below me. When the first light of morning hit these landscapes, if God permitted or if I were still alive, I would search for them.

Chapter 31

I had a terrible night, jumping, itching, covered with ants, bees, slugs, flies, bugs, lice and aphids. Gigantic grubs and alien mealworms and crispy wasp larvae had captured me near the castle of termites on the northern side of Mposi Campus and had imprisoned me in the snails' holes. I could not move. They asked me a lot of questions—where I had come from, who had given me authorization to eat their sisters and brothers, etc. And they punished me physically and mentally with delicious smoky steak salad, grilled Asian marinated fat ribs, layers of chicken fajitas, with juicy shrimp, lobster with wild beans, pot roast le French, warm potato salad platters, pumpkin chocolate chip pancakes, pot BBQ pulled pork, and hundreds and hundreds of other dishes.

They laughed.

I heard their laughter from solitary confinement, and I was able to see them as human beings, dressed in green, making me cut plants with my teeth, and during all those infinite hours I spent another seven hours cleaning their mess. During this period, I attempted to escape several times. I could not, resulting in my legs not belonging to me any longer.

I screamed.

They kept laughing.

But, suddenly, I escaped, just to fall into this gully, where Rudolph Guerra, Ranjit Sandhu, Josh Hansel, Miguel Bojorquez, and Dieng Chung, dressed as termites and snails, chased me, with funny bounces, from the sides of the ponds.

I ran.

I recognized I was running in a circle.

Leave me alone, please!

Look! He's crying. Mr. Junior is crying!

Ha! Ha! Ha!

There were those nightmarish slugs. I became one. I was climbing up the sugarcane plants and, at the time, I saw myself seeking a way to escape.

However, I couldn't.

I saw them in front of me. Colonel de Mposi had become a bee.

Then a dream took me backward, to my friend Ernest. However, his companions were not the regular folks of the Club of Bsar. Rather, they had the facial features of bullet-headed skulls. Others had egg-shaped heads or were hydrocephalic or microcephalic. They sat at the table, eating mealworms and snails alive, and there were Judith and Meredith, from whose mouths maggots were coming out as they were eating, and I ran again.

Just to fall into this thick pond of larvae, and I started drowning.

Chapter 32

I subsequently escaped, and when I woke up it was still dark but I would not dare to go back to sleep.

Yet I began to learn. I remembered the guys. Ab: "A body covered with mud will make the insects go away and cure ant bites." He had done it to my hands, so I did the same to my body. As far I could tell, my body had been attacked with all kinds of teeth, but I was still standing.

When I finished, I served myself a mealworm and wasp larvae breakfast, and I began the exploration, carefully, eyes open, aware of where I was putting my feet, wary of snakes, black scorpions, wandering spiders and the scariest, the big cats.

Chapter 33

Nothing is going to keep me from reaching civilization, and I am determined to do so.

William Rockefeller said it.

I believed him.

Making the most of the early light of the morning, and what I had learned so far on the campus of Mposi was the instinct of survival. I took the easy trail to see everything from right to left.

Was I walking in the rainforest, alongside trees and among wild animals and dangerous lizards and insects? The answer is yes—but this part of the trail did not require me to use the machete, because I could see. So all I need to do was look out until I reached a spot from where I could go below to the canyon. In fact, it was not a canyon. It was, rather, an enormous terrain.

There was a clean, green passage, and the beauty of the extraordinary landscape was unforgettable. It made me wonder how it was possible that they had planted this sugarcane field in the middle of nowhere.

There had to be a purpose that would answer all the questions, I hoped. Was my father part of this sinister plan? Was he connected to Colonel de Mposi or Mr. Guerra?

I doubted it.

Well, I didn't know, but what I knew was that they had chosen a place and no one was prepared for it.

From the Bahamas to this—that was something to think about.

I moved on. Wary of unexpected things.

Now and then I stopped. I scanned my surroundings, where the bushlands on the slopes were so thick and so human-looking that they made me look twice.

I couldn't see the sun but I was sure it was behind the higher hills or mountains, where the trees blocked its rays.

The clear ground was gone and the nature trail had disappeared as well. It made me wonder—should I venture to the massive curtain of the rainforest or keep going along this narrow pathway without knowing where it would end? I was undecided and there was no one whom I could depend upon to play tic-tac-toe with for an answer.

I grasped my machete.

Ahead, the pathway was narrower, and bushes, twisted trunks and fallen branches were all over it. I could see spoiled red fruits, hundreds of them, on the ground.

Then, suddenly, I heard the noises of monkeys, half-way up the trees on which they were jumping and bouncing, and that made me halt to watch them leap from one tree to another and display their sharp teeth. Far above me, they were leaping over the branches, making me very nervous. Just as I started walking, with the intention of going back, a brown-green cat looked at me, holding a monkey in his teeth. Momentarily paralyzed, ready to defend myself at any cost, I started jogging a little. I needed to control any negative emotion to get out of there alive.

Ahead, I could see only trees, hills, mountains and the stunning seal of nature.

The good thing was that I heard the sound of water. Where was it coming from?

I did not know. I edged along the terrain, carefully looking for firm ground on the other side. Just then, I saw a movement. It was not something I was expecting: a large snake, with its stiletto-like tongue jerking in and out, straightened up, hanging from a branch. I pressed the machete, ready. I could face it. Above, I detected another action. I seemed like a part of the jungle's morning meal. Sharp as the blade, the snake attacked me.

I cut the snake, but the jaguar made me scream and lose balance.

On Mposi Campus, Ares was the first to wake up, as had been his habit since he had arrived at the place. He urinated behind the barracks and took a shower under the tank, where the water was as cold as ice. Drying his body against the wind, he prepared fire for the coffee and the morning breakfast, which consisted of leftovers from dinner—bullfrogs, snakes and the delicacy, rabbits.

Ab found him the coffee powder that had been recycled five times. He asked him about the new assignments, where, after the afternoon quotation, they would go hunting for food and, most importantly, if there would be another plan to escape. He and Ab appeared to understand the value of their names and experience of this place. But Ab was still very disappointed about the whole thing—his name, his father and what he had become.

"We're buried here, and there is no way to write to him or send a report of what we have achieved."

"Have we learned enough to be unburied?"

"We have."

"They don't think so."

Sol and Gil and Popo joined the group, just as the coffee was being made.

"We need to get some supplies from the Amazon Supermarket."

"Me and Ares were thinking about it."

It was then that Sol and Gil went quiet for a moment, an act of respect each one of them noticed. For Sol, every day was a Memorial Day for his sister, Carmen, the brightest member of the Kuo family, a kind of genius who, by her fourteenth birthday, was a senior at the University of Oxford. But she was killed in the summertime by a drunkard, a block from Plaza Tormer. In Gil's case, it was his grandmother. He spoke about her as if she was alive, and he had told us, "If she were alive, I tell you, I wouldn't be here."

He was here.

She had died ten years ago, when he was only eight years old.

After they ate, they sat there, but this time Ares was a little talkative.

"I miss that fool."

They knew who he was talking about.

"We should pray for him."

"He will not make it."

Ares spoke again.

"We need to plan it right."

"Think about something?"

"Yes, Sol. This time, we need to study their movements and those monthly deliveries. We have never thought about them."

"What if our fathers have been thinking about our decision and experience?" Gil observed. "Is this a lesson or a punishment that deserves to be reversed?"

"It should be," Popo replied, "but we don't know how to approach it. As we can see, there is no way to communicate with them."

"I have been here four years," Ares said. "And I think for myself there is a point. We made a mistake, and others have made several. I cannot blame Rocko. Does my father have a thought about me? A single thought? The last time I saw him was behind the Adgain and then he sat in the back of the limo. How pitiful!"

"I agree."

"Me, too."

"I'm with Ares."

"So am I."

"That's the truth."

"I think Rocko has been thinking the same thing, and without knowing the truth of this matter, he decided to dig into the colonel's background."

They fell into silence again.

Chapter 34

I fell over trees, rocks and then mud. That I did not die because of that fall was a miracle. I was alive, but I did not know how many bones were broken and needed to be fixed. Each had a different sense of pain, and the most lacerating was the pain in my ribcage.

I was able to see where I was—not in the hole, but firmly in the ground.

I got to my knees and looked around. Not much to see because of the thick bushlands and layers of trees and roots. I had lost my machete and, in pain and feeling messed up, I began to look for it.

After minutes of exasperation, I found it several feet from a gigantic setup of roots. I tried to hold on for a few moments, but a spider made me rise. I killed it while I was getting up. I peeped at my right leg, then my left arm, which was kind of twisted, and I fixed it as far as I could. I used my belt, and it was then that I began to see I was in a bad situation.

Chapter 35

I stood up amidst the green branches that were bent over and the bushlands and let my mind take me from those pains for a while. It was dark, even though I felt the sun over the canopies of the higher trees. I was not in screaming pain. I was still hot, and ready, and my body had not lost its energy, and yet my chest, both sides of my body, my legs, arms and the entire spectrum of me needed medical attention.

There was no road, no avenue to move freely along, and the walls were made up of trees, roots and bushes, entwined and too massive to pass through. Rain started pouring. Heavy drops, as if they were projectiles. I found no place to hide, and I was alone, sharing my loneliness with giant centipedes, wandering spiders, scorpions and slippery snakes. I could not will myself to disappear. I had to deal with them carefully.

I halted.

Sounds?

Did I hear those sounds?

Were those sounds?

There was the sound of the rain, but I began to hear all kinds of other sounds. They were now closer, and then those eyes.

Chapter 36

It took more than a month for me to see the red face of the woman, and a week to understand that I was still in the forest, an Amazonian place. I was within the same perimeter I had left before.

I wasn't a geography genius who knew the faces of Indians, except from social media and from almost-forgotten textbooks of history, but I noticed I was in an Indian village, 100 kilometers from the Mposi compound, lying in a hammock. They had cured my body with mashed green leaves and stones, and I was healthy and my body had got a lot of energy.

The air of recognition passed through the windowless house. Above, a grass roof was the most attractive decoration I saw in the entire place.

The brawny woman was active. She spoke a language it was impossible to grasp. A man, almost naked as she was, came in and with him a second man, younger than him, with the same characteristics. He spoke. I could not understand what he was saying. He glanced at me, and then backed up. The younger one tried to communicate in his language and mine. He turned and left the room, as the other had done.

Chapter 37

A strange welcome.

In the course of 14 days, I recovered sufficiently from my injuries to get out of the hammock and venture outside the house, where, for a little while, I enjoyed knowing the woman who had watched over me, her husband, their son and many more, but none of them had the ability to tell me where civilization was.

I kept asking them where the big city was.

Communication with them was impossible. I had read about the uncontacted people in the Amazon rainforest— the indigenous peoples in Brazil, such as Poros indígenas no Brasil, the isolated groups, or the loggers or the Kolina, with their cannibalistic rituals—and now I could not distinguish between them.

I walked around the village, trying to find someone who could understand me, but I was out of luck. What did I expect? My presence was not a cause for distraction or curiosity to them, which was clear from the way they were doing their things, and nothing indicated that I was a danger to them.

At dinner time, I sat by a fire. A man was cooking a monkey, roots, fishes and fruits over it. I addressed the woman who had attended to me.

"Where is the town?"

I made all kinds of signals with my fingers and palms, trying to make her understand what I wanted.

She just smiled, handing me a chunk of monkey meat and some roots in a leaf.

She made a gesture.

Eat.

What happened next, I didn't expect. Her son, surrounded by his wife and children and other relatives, stretched out his arm with a sophisticated mug made up of leaves. It contained a dark, heavy liquor that made me close my eyes when I tasted it. I communicated with him with the movements of my hands.

Instead of answering, he shook his hands, sending a message I was able to decode.

In the following minutes, I didn't know what happened. I had eaten, and, wandering in the village, I felt as if I were a hunted bird.

When I came to, I was in Mposi.

Chapter 38

My presence, how I had I got in and who had brought me—the boys returning to the barracks did not make a big deal of it, and it was like I had never left the Mposi compound. There were no questions about what had happened back there in the jungle and why I was here. Instead of that, Sol and Gil asked me if I was hungry or if I needed something from them.

Ab saluted me as if I were in the sugarcane fields, as did Popo, Al, Big, Jet, Eyes and But, and when Ares had put food away for the next morning, he came over to me, while I was still in the hammock.

"Tomorrow we're going to shop at the Amazon Supermarket. You're welcome to come with us."

I sensed no bad feelings, no curiosity about what I had done or how I had come back to this hole. Did he, as well as the others, understand my dilemma? So what was the purpose of repeating the same failure?

"I almost died back there, Ares."

"You tried."

Getting out of the hammock, I sat across it, balancing myself as he was balanced on his.

"They appear to know. Is this a setup from which there is no escape?"

He glared at me. I wanted to speak, tell him I had been wrong, and I would not accept the fact that everyone above us wanted us to see that they controlled us and could do whatever they pleased because we had made a mistake and had been blind. "I will not take it as a defeat. I just can't."

He didn't speak.

In the silence, I felt a sense of loneliness that I had never dreamed of filling my young chest. I jumped to the floor, and, moving my injured arm too fast, I screamed with anger. The few residents of the barracks watched me as I moved out. Ares was next to me, but he was quiet.

"I'm a rich boy and I can see my life may end here. How I hate my father, man!"

"We must find out the truth."

"How?"

He stepped out of the muddy ground and stood near a low table, holding edible plants, not yet ready to be eaten, that belonged to Eyes.

"By facing the illogical pathway and being smart, Rocko. Why we are here and what we have learned? First, is this a punishment from an old man or from our mother, and how long can we endure?"

"Do they know?"

"To be honest, they know, as we are valued assets and whether we die or not has consequences. It's up to us."

"What is the conclusion here, Ares?"

"The same that our father and mother want us to perceive and we're too blind to admit."

Chapter 39

I sat in the office of Colonel de Mposi. He came in alone for the first time.

He picked up a cigar made from a turtle shell and lit it. "How was your trip?"

"You seem to enjoy this psychological torture."

"On the contrary, Mr. Rockefeller."

"What did you call it?"

"Momentum of truth, a kind of assimilation."

"I see."

"Do you really see it, Mr. Rockefeller?"

"To be honest, I don't."

"It's time you or others must."

"I won't."

"You will see."

"Yeah."

Mr. de Mposi shrugged his shoulders.

Guerra made his appearance.

"We expect rain."

"We need to get a bit strict around here. This wanderer here, his quota will be 4,000 for six months."

"You aren't going to break me."

"Of course not, Mr. Rockefeller, but the sugarcane fields will."

They stared at me.

"Four thousand monthly is a lot of cutting, Rocko," Sol said.

"They want to see you straight," Al observed.

"We can help, uh, Ares? Ab, you help him with the preparation of his food."

"They will be aware of that. And that will be hard for us."

I was not worried about not meeting my monthly quota. I was quiet and listening to them. Popo wrapped up a fried snake. "We can do the cuts after Mr. Guerra takes a break."

"Don't worry, guys."

"You need to see the truth, Rocko."

Chapter 40

I returned to the sugarcane fields. The Black Shadow had told me that I needed to reach 4,000 pounds. I grasped with force the machete when I was in the widened pathway and held it steady with my fingers. I stared at him. He stared back. I had no feeling in my face.

The boys (Gil, Al, Sol, Ares, Eyes, But, Ab) watched on. After a while, I noticed he backed up, not defeated, shaking his head.

"You're going to do that alone. No pairs."

"You will have your damned quota, Master Chief."

"I am not your enemy here, Mr. Rockefeller."

I moved down the narrow trail to the site, where the sugarcane plants were taller than palm trees.

Ares communicated with gestures and hands. "Don't let them see you fighting against your own shadows."

I replied, "I just did, Ares."

Then I ignored his second message.

The sun was above me.

I was cutting sugarcane roots. I was ahead of Ares, Sol, Ab and Eyes. They were the young masters of cutting, but I was still angry at what my father had done. My sisters and brothers. My friends and those I presumed loved me.

The sound of the break.

I didn't stop to eat my mid-day meat. The hatred made me strong.

The more I thought about this hatred that was inside me, the gladder I was that I didn't allow them to see me beg. I didn't expect to get any pity if I tried to escape again. This was probably an experiment to see me suffer, and even if I was guilty (though I was not) of causing Vernis' death or Meredith's mutation, I'd never go to give up my name as a sissy boy.

While I was thinking about that, Witz made his presence felt once more with his entourage. I was ahead of the others, and Ares was the closest to me. I was alone, but this time I was not going to run. I would choose to face him.

"You own me, pretty boy. Remember? You're alone now and my boys here are going to enjoy you, too."

Edward "Col" Colmman and Bryan "Vill" Villarroel formed a circle around me.

"You're very pretty wet."

There were rasping chuckles and laughs.

Jerry "Yum" Yuan and Norwin "Win" Sparza echoed them, and while Armand "Ass" Assayag ambled to the right, trying to cut off my rear, I didn't wait. I slid a sugarcane root off the side of the machete, threw it away and then held the machete out elegantly. It was a shock to Witz and the others that I made this move bluntly in front of him, since he was considered not the biggest but the toughest leader on campus. In fact, Witz was a strong and mean boy, a bully, who was the son of Frank M. Markowitz, CEO and President of Herspert Company, a solid platform for the export of Saudi Arabian gas.

This time, he received three shocking hits. Left and right. Back and front, making him cry out, while Ass and Win backed up. As I hit them simultaneously, I did not give them any chance to strike me back.

Yet I was alone, receiving here and there a bit of pain, and, because my arm was not strong enough, I began to feel it.

Yu and Col made their move. I broke that move with several sugarcane roots against their bodies. It seemed my unexpected attack had made them lose energy, especially Witz, who was bleeding.

Clearly, I was ahead of him, their leader. My machete landed flat on Witz' back. He howled in pain.

Ares, Sol, Gil, An and Al ran towards us.

"Hey, Rocko! No! Rocko!"

I straightened up before them like a victorious Roman gladiator. Witz was kneeling, and he understood.

"Are you alright, Rocko?"

"I'm good."

Witz saw my determination. He nodded. Yu and Vill came over to him and helped him get up.

As they lifted him, I stepped forward. The others sought refuge behind the defeated leader.

"You ever come to me with a proposal... hear me?"

"Got it."

"You bet."

Ares thought about the way I handled things as he approached me.

"Cool, right?"

"Cool."

I was standing in the marked lane of Barrack One. It was late afternoon when Mr. Guerra checked and examined the piles of sugarcane roots while having a word with Sugarcane Field Overseer Carlito Gaver or, as we called him, Master Field Gaver.

After having confirmed that there were 4,000, he found me next to Ares, Sol, Ab and Al and the other boys of Barrack One.

"You guys go to formation," said Mr. Guerra. As they moved to the narrow trail, to be ready to move to the barracks, he glanced at me. "What happened with Witz?"

"I put him in his place, Master Chief."

"How did you feel?"

"I felt nothing, Master Chief."

He nodded.

"Get in line. You're done."

When I returned to the barracks, I found Josh Hansel standing across the plaza of Mposi, where the pathway provided access to the barracks and the main population.

"Hey, Rocko, where are you going? We need to go hunting."

"Give me a sec, Ares."

Josh Hansel was not alone. He was with Col, Vill, Win, Ass and Witz. I approached him and I did not salute him as Master Chief, and I said, "There is no law in Mposi and I can do whatever I please to each one of you."

"How dare you, boy! I am a Master Chief."

"You're just a piece of shit."

"You will not want to have a war with me, pretty princess."

"I am ready to have it."

"Mr. Rockefeller, back to your barracks. I'm ready to count."

"Yes, Master Chief."

We (Ares, Popo, Sol, Ab, Al and I) were hunting. Popo was very good at getting rabbits, snakes, possums and edible rodents, while Ares was skilled at making traps for big animals such as wild boars, monkeys and other edible wild animals. Sol had become a specialist in finding edible plants, such as tamarind, wild pistachio, abal, dandelion, wild rose, almond, agave, canna lily, manioc, papaya, cattail, batoko, amaranth, asparagus, chestnut, bearberry, acorns, jujube, fishtail, date palm, sweetsop and many more. Sol could spot edible roots, wild potatoes, beans and beets, and Ab and Al could spot spices. I began to learn what Ares taught me, guessing I was part of the circle, but I expected to show my skill at fishing. Perhaps because I loved the sea.

But they always advised me against going after the dangerous fish of the Amazon River, which was a hundred miles from the campus. I recognized that that side of the campus was unknown to me, but not to them.

There was a reason no one from the campus had dared to venture to that side. It consisted of more than 500 kilometers of water infested with bull sharks, red-bellied piranhas, electric eels, black caimans, great white sharks and other lethal creatures.

Ares told me that, if there was no boat, the chances of surviving were zero, and you could not swim as far as a bull shark.

I told him that I was considering building one. He just smiled at me.

We saw some kids of the Mposi hunting across the dark lake, challenging those magnificent black caimans, while we (especially I) began to see more.

Across the water, this landscape was civilization, my world.

After a while we'd lost track of the hours and did not know how many minutes late we returned to the compound. It all seemed like a festival. The boys were cooking, reserving food and making it available to the other kids of our circle. Other kids traded and exchanged food with other residents.

Me—I never forgot that new track of paradise across the river, not north or south, but west, if I considered the geographical region of Mposi and where I had come from to this place. It would then be far west.

That was indeed on the opposite side of the campus.

Chapter 41

Over the course of late September and throughout December, while much of the Mposi residents' attention was on the stormy rain causing devastation, hardly a day passed in Barrack One without a conversation about getting to the other side of the river, planning among us or stories from those who had tried to cross the river, which could be useful for us in the future.

We chilled in a corner of the barracks, drinking wild ground cacao seeds. Gil made a paste out of them, liquid enough to drink, and it was hot. Master Chiefs did not call the residents of the barracks out to be counted because of the rain, and Colonel de Mposi had agreed to let us stay away from the sugarcane fields because of nature's fury.

We had a lot of time to think.

In the morning, we (Ares, Sol, Popo and Gil) came out of the barracks. Under the rain, we crossed the plaza, from a site not seen by the overseers or the man himself, Colonel de Mposi. We discovered that this part was large and sloped. The deep terrain seemed to be cut off from the mainland. It was not bad if you knew where to go.

Ares and I spent more time than the others observing these unknown gullies and canyons and then seeking a route for our escape, because the place was built up high. Even though the rain and darkness made it impossible to get a clear picture, I recognized from that side a narrow road. Water from the high mountain overflowed over it with force.

We saw Sol, Popo and Gil ahead of us.

"We left you guys behind."

Popo pointed at a ditch.

"That trail takes us this way."

"Really? Show it to us."

Ares and I followed Popo, Sol and Gil, who were leading us.

The compound was always to our right. Popo halted.

"Be careful."

We had to, because of the depth of the terrain. We ambled to it, grasping bushes and trunks.

"There."

Ares and I recognized the trail and then the narrow road from where I had reached Mposi. That remembrance hit them as well.

"Could this be the way to civilization?"

I looked at Gil. "If it is, it is a long way to get there."

"I remember. Yes, the jeep, horses and travelling by foot."

The narrow road had to take us somewhere. I communicated, and we followed the road. One thousand feet and the campus was gone from our vision, and we realized that this was the main way to reach Mposi. I pushed myself forward. They followed me. I looked around, to get details, and even though the rain made it difficult, I felt I was on track. It seemed so familiar, but I just couldn't place it. Was it the same road? I communicated my thoughts to them. They did not remember either.

At this time, the entire place was at the mercy of the rain. The road became narrower, and we stopped. In front of us was a crater, and it was more than 100 kilometers to the other side.

"This isn't the way, Rocko."

"It seems so."

"Let us go around its edge," Sol suggested.

"There must be another way. What do you think, Ares?"

Ares replied, "The rain makes it impossible, Sol."

"Let us do what Gil has said."

"We don't have our machetes, Rocko."

"Ares is right, Rocko."

"What next?"

"We come back. We know now."

We returned, undressed, changed into dry clothes and sat in our corner. Popo told Al and Ab what we had found and, after that, we kept to ourselves. But we were attentive to any suggestions. We were sure we were on top of a hill or a slope. Sol and Popo disagreed.

"Let us presume we are not, but from now on, we should keep our eyes open when we come to the plaza. We will see a difference."

That made them think.

Al got an idea. "We can find that answer in Colonel de Mposi's office."

"How is that going to happen? That office is his home."

Silence.

"We see him in the morning and the evening," I said. "That's it. I do expect he's a mystery man and we never question that servant. Is she a server, or a lover, a watcher? We never see her out of that office."

More mysteries.

"What do you suggest, Rocko?"

"Find out anything about this place, and Colonel de Mposi has to have a map or something. "

"You agree with what Al has said."

"I do."

"Ares?"

"I am with Rocko. We've found more information during this rain than during three years here."

"Alright. I am in."

Every one of us agreed.

"The question is, who has the balls to do it?"

"I will make it happen."

"I will go with you, Rocko."

"Then we're going to plan it. We have to watch the Master Chiefs."

We began to plan our movements. We made two plans. Sol, Popo, Gil and Ab focused on Mr. Matle Sandhou—the colonel's assistant—and Miss Borzaga, allowing Ares and me to enter the office.

While this was being discussed, Master Chief Guerra surprised us, eating wild berries and, without saying a word, saluted each one of us and got our names for the afternoon counting routine in the field. He even told us that if it continued raining the next day, he would find some activities for us. He could see that would be difficult to venture outside in this weather. We kept quiet. We were ready.

Chapter 42

Mr. Matle Sandhou was more than an assistant.

He had a small cottage next to the Colonel of Mposi's main house, accessed by a bridge, where a series of Cape Cod cottages were built low as protection against the heavy wind and the rainforest. The Master Chiefs lived there, as did Alejandro Sánchez, who, during the rainy season, had not come out of his cottage. According to Sol's report, and later from Gil's observations, it would be up to us (Ares and me) to verify the best way to enter into Colonel's house.

Sol saw Colonel of Mposi moving to the main house in the morning. At about eight o'clock, he came out and had a meeting with all the Master Chiefs. Sol wasn't able to figure out what they were talking about, and he, Popo or Gil, could not move freely to reach the Office House.

By twelve, with the rain continuing, he came out. He moved back to the cottage to prepare himself for the rain with a yellow waterproof coat, boots and hat. He reached the pathway protected by a rocky wall and kept walking. Sol had problems following him, and he could not communicate with Popo or Gil. He tried to circle the cottage, but he was afraid to be seen by Alejandro or anyone from the main house.

"And?"

"Nothing. I've been waiting. So far, I haven't seen him."

Ares and I were quiet. We knew for a fact that that side was impossible to venture to. It had been 24 hours since any of us had seen him.

From the distance of the main office house, Popo had seen Sol. It was then that he ran behind Barrack Three, came up before the plaza, dropped himself into the small ditch, now filled with water, and examined the office of Colonel de Mposi.

For hours, he had witnessed a meeting led by Mr. Sandhou, and he had noted the absence of the man himself—Colonel de Mposi.

Later, when he told us, our question was, "Have you seen Mr. Mposi?"

"I am telling you guys, no. And when the Black Shadow Ru went back again, he closed the door."

We were silent.

It was confirmed by Gil, who had been watching the right wing of the office. We were thinking hard. We reached the conclusion that he was sick or doing his thing with Miss Borzaga. It's nature. We were men and humans.

"When will you move in?"

"After we eat."

The rain stopped for a few minutes, and then it came back stronger than before. Our territory had begun to feel the rain, and the ground had had enough. The day became darker quickly and this offered us a good shield under which to move directly from our barracks to the office of Mr. Mposi. A Mposi resident kid passed by. He had stolen meat from someone. Ares recognized him and he told him he belonged to Barrack Three.

Off the left wing of Mr. Mposi's office, in the site's exclusive zone for Cape Cod cottages, Alejandro Sánchez watched out of the window, smoking, scanning, like an eagle. Touching Ares' shoulder, I brought his attention to Mr. Sánchez.

He nodded.

We did not move. The standoff that followed drew us from watching Mr. Sánchez to contemplating the mysterious disappearance of Mr. Sandhou as well as the rare absence of Mr. Mposi.

Alejandro Sánchez then opened the window and tossed the cigarette butt out and closed it. We reacted, too. With careful steps, we walked to the rear door and climbed the 20 steps.

The view from here was impressive. Handling the watching well, Ares signaled that it was okay. I moved alone through the outdoor corridor to the window and peeped in. It was dark, and it appeared empty.

He shook his head, moved cautiously to the door and opened it. Then he communicated using his hands—"Nobody in." and "Do I wait?"—and by that time I was next to him. We stepped in.

We moved into the hall that linked the kitchen, the rooms and his domain, where he received the kids under him.

"You look on that side."

"Yeah."

We began to search inside the cabinets and shelves. A few minutes later, we halted on the other side of the office. These cabinets and drawers were empty.

"What is going on?"

I looked again around the office, and Ares took another look in the rooms. I halted near the window that faced Alejandro's cottage.

"Perhaps we're looking in the wrong places."

"This is the office."

"Sure."

"What is it?"

"He may have another place to hide what we are looking for."

"The handler, Alejandro?"

"Yeah."

"We need another plan, Rocko."

"Certainly."

"Let us plan it more carefully."

A plan was made to search Alejandro's cottage at night. We felt confident and in full control of what we were doing.

"Let us be careful."

We were not familiar with the parcel, even though it was inside the perimeter of Mposi. We walked easily along the avenue of rocks and bushlands and massive trees. We handled the machete occasionally, so as not to make a mess or to alert others to our presence. Through the rainforest world we went until we came to a wall as a result of which the pathway did not go any further. We were able to distinguish a cave with an iron door and it was clear that there was something hidden in there.

"Are you thinking what I am thinking, Ares?"

"A treasure?"

"More."

We could not break the lock, and this caused us a moment of vacillation. When we returned to the barracks, we learned that Big was a master of breaking locks. This made sense. His father was Alexander Cruz, the CEO of UnLock Company, the one who created the unbreakable code lock <<Criz 17>>, which, Big, with his friends, had decoded for fun, believe it or not. He was here because of that, a father's punishment to a son whose actions had cost him more than 87 million dollars.

"It's a garage," Big observed.

Two cars were missing. The spaces were marked.

I glanced at Ares. "Can you understand it? They have a garage."

"It's clear now that Mposi or Sandhou have gone somewhere."

"How can we take it, Rocko?"

Rain continued pouring.

I looked around, finding everything we needed for a long stay, and then I came out of the cave. I looked around. I wanted to get behind that locked door but I couldn't. I had plenty of time to discover the hill road and, below it, an unknown inroad.

"This is another way to get down there, Ares, and we are going to find it."

Chapter 43

It was a perfect but ugly night. There were doubts over whether we had chosen the perfect time to get inside Alejandro's place. It was easy to get in, thanks to Big. We found the cottage huge and high and quite clear, except the living room and dining room. We found a pair of snakes in a cage and the head of a caiman hanging from the ceiling.

A table. On top of it, a plate with pieces of yucca and pork and a half-bottle of homemade rum and a notebook.

I picked up the notebook.

He was lying in bed. Snoring. Wrapped up in the same clothes we saw him in every day. Strangely enough, we saw a photo from which a woman and a child stared at us. His clothes hung in pairs from hangers on the ceiling. There was nothing else in the room except this reports, logs, and names of kids and other residents who had lived here previously. We found CURRENT REPORTS in all the barracks. The Master Chiefs had written about the behaviors of the residents and there were reports about many kids missing, dead. I found my reports from day one. CHANGES & ASSIMILATIONS—when I began to adapt, to follow orders. From handwritten notes: "restless, touchy, strong, but good, learning quickly"—Mr. Guerra, and with the initials of Colonel de Mposi.

I felt Ares' hand on my shoulders. He indicated a section of the room. More than 100 boxes were piled up. Big had already separated a couple of boxes—BARRACK ONE & POST OFFICE. Big took out letters from these boxes as well as postcards. They were unopened, stamped and sealed. I saw Ares fall to the floor, holding several letters. Big was seated. I was afraid of seeing more. I had to. It took me a while to find the letters from my sisters, Cherlyn and Lorraine. There was more. I stumbled through letters addressed to Al, Gil, Ab, Sol and others.

How dare they?

I was livid at the conduct of the Master Chiefs and Colonel de Mposi. It had caused alarm among us. We had realized that they knew about our fathers' existences or what we and our families were, and Ares and I had decided to come to Alejandro's cottage at night to search his place. Attempts would also be made to go through the other Master Chiefs' places if we were unable to find what we were looking for.

Now, before the examination all of these letters and reports, we were speechless.

I looked at Ares. He was crying, and Big did not know what to do, pacing up and down, saying, "This is unfair." Similarly, that was the reaction I had until my eyes fell on those boxes.

MONTHLY LOG, by Colonel de Mposi.

I took it.

"Are we going to take all of these, Rocko, and distribute them to the kids? They belong to them."

"They will know someone has entered this garage, Big."

"I don't care. If they find out, I will take the full responsibility."

"It isn't about that, Big. We're after something more solid. The map of the place. We can all leave together."

"Alright, Rocko. Got it. So, you two go ahead. I'll close it."

I peeped at Ares. He was already standing up.

"Are you alright with that, Ares?"

"Yeah."

"Be careful, Big."

"Get this, and I am good Rocko."

Outside the cottage, we exchanged looks, but we did not speak. When we returned, the boys were waiting for us. I let Ares tell them what we had found. He was able to deliver two or three letters to them. We received the same reaction from Sol, Popo, Gil, Ab, Al and Jet that we had had when we had discovered the letters. In silence, they moved to their hammocks. I lay in my hammock. But vague images reached me—my father, our long discussion, his frustration, my mother's death because of him, had left me questioning what true love was.

Were these Master Chiefs aware of these reports and letters, most importantly Colonel de Mposi? What if I died back there or here? What if I started, in fear, to perform aggressive actions towards myself or others?

But I had survived like the other kids, making our lives count every day.

Later in the evening, Ares told me, after he had read the letters of his mother, that there was a growing belief among his family members that he was going to survive through these parcels of sugarcanes and that all these were types of survival tools that would be good for him and would improve his social skills. "They're certain I'll grow because of all the difficulties, including my father, whom I saw that day in the court, unsmiling," he remembered. "How ironic that sounds! Is this love or a new way of punishment? I don't get it, and now, as I read the letters of Mum and how happy she and he are, I am doing fine."

I made the most of this opportune time, when very few of us were focusing on what we had achieved, by reading the monthly log of Colonel de Mposi and his observations and the responses to our fathers and mothers.

They listened carefully. His writing was not for the court but, rather, to our fathers and mothers. "He has been reporting about us."

"Like an experiment on caged animals," Sol muttered between his teeth. "Mr. Mposi's actions are so sick, man."

"Perhaps," Al said, but he didn't go further.

Popo began asking me aggressively if we weren't going to challenge Mposi's rights. "He doesn't have the right to do what he was doing, as it is unheard of and brutal, Macko. We must challenge him."

I didn't respond to Popo's anger. My mind was still.

"Are we going to step aside from our plan?"

Each one of them spoke.

"No, Rocko," Ab replied. "We know now."

"Then that is what I want to hear."

A few minutes later, we saw Big enter the barracks. He was cool, and when we asked about what he had promised, his reply was a dry, "Yeah."

We fell silent. We heard the rain.

When later we ate our last meals of the day, the barracks was dark, and we hurried to lie in our hammocks.

I heard the sound of rain. I heard the sound of the creatures here and there, and the hunters, the rainforest ghosts.

Chapter 44

"What happened?"

"Wake up! Wake up!"

"What is going on?"

"Get up and move out! Now!"

"It's still raining, Master Chief."

"Do I care? Move out!"

I did not know what the time was. It was early, not even three. Ares looked at me.

"Any idea?"

I shook my head.

Mr. Guerra's voice boomed again. He stormed along the corridor with a torch. A minute later, Ares, Sol, Ab, Gil, Popo, Al and I dashed out into the rain. The residents of the other barracks were there too, and we did not notice Mr. Sandhou or Alejandro Sánchez. Master Chiefs gathered and were talking amongst themselves in the middle of the plaza, which was overflowing with water.

"Are they commanding us to go to sugarcane fields?"

"That would be crazy."

"I won't go."

"Listen up, ladies!" Mr. Guerra's voice was heard. "Someone among you has broken into Overseer Sánchez' cottage and removed some valuable things from it."

"Ask him. He may need whatever it was to feed rabbits in the jungle," one of the kids said.

"He's missing."

Ares and I exchanged looks, and slowly, we glanced in the direction of Big. He peeped at us and shrugged his shoulders.

"Let us talk. Otherwise, no one is going to sleep tonight."

That was a promise.

Three hours later, we were still standing in the rain. Some kids could not stand up and called for it to stop. The Master Chiefs were determined to find out about the boxes in Sánchez' cottage.

Ares signaled to Big that he should change places with Eyes and But. He did. Ares whispered to him. I leaned over.

"What happened back at Alejandros' cottage, Big?"

"Nothing."

"We're together."

"I know, Ares."

I pressed him. "You won't lie to us."

"We're brothers of blood. I couldn't."

But I kept pressing him, assuming a Rockefeller's attitude. Many of the kids knew he was lying and was not a good man.

"Eventually, we're going to know what happened back there."

He nodded. "I took all those boxes and I hid them in a place."

"You shouldn't have done that, Big."

"Alejandro?"

"He was still sleeping."

I looked into his eyes and tapped his shoulders.

"Okay."

The punishment was still on.

The rain had stopped temporarily. Behind the foggy horizon, the sun wanted to come out.

Master Chief Bojorquez approached Master Chief Guerra. He spoke with him, and Ab read his lips.

"What is he saying?"

"He wants to get some coffee."

Master Chief Guerra nodded, and Master Chief Miguel Bojorques turned and kicked the muddy ground to go to their privileged kitchen a few feet from the main office, but he couldn't pass through. Water had invaded the flat terrain and the small bridge had vanished. It was a little deep; in summertime, a hundred colorful fish from the lake and wild roses populated it.

He edged around the place. The water reached him no matter what precautions he took, but he made it to the side. Casually, like everyone in the barracks, he watched for dangerous snakes or wild animals. He halted. He wanted to be sure.

After that, he called Master Chief Guerra.

"Rudolph, you have to see this."

They found Alejandro Sánchez with his throat cut and 10 stab wounds in his body that had resulted from a knife or a similar pointed object. He was completely naked.

Chapter 45

For the next week and a half, the death of Alejandro Sánchez was a sensation and a mystery in the Mposi compound and Ares andI did not hold back from having a word with Big, walking around the barracks. He explained in detail to us where he had hidden the boxes with the intention of burning them. Changing his mind, he had left the cottage a quarter of an hour before the last calls of the Master Chiefs, which would be around twelve.

"I saw Mr. Guerra patrolling the place and then I returned."

Big and his friend Buthad reached this place together and had told us about But's sister, Amelin, who had died of cancer last year, which was known by the Master Chiefs and Colonel de Mposi, who had arranged a trip for him to visit his family, which would be the end of his time in Mposi. He gave that assignment to Alejandro Sánchez, but when Master Chief Sánchez had tried to take advantage of him, Greg "Big" Cruz reacted aggressively, and his three hundred pounds of solid muscle had sent Master Chief Sánchez to his death.

"He had passed the line of trust, man. I needed to stand up."

"I do understand, Big, but—"

"No, man. That has nothing to do with what happened to him now, Rocko. When Mom pushed me out of her belly, she pushed a man. And I will stay that way or I will die."

We felt Big's voice, and we took a few minutes to swallow the new situation.

I spoke. "Someone has been watching him or us."

"What did you say? One of the Mposi kids has killed him?"

"Yes, Big. If he tried to rape you, he must have done it successfully with other kids. We have dozens of kids here who don't have our strength or trust or a way to survive, and he may have taken advantage of that."

"Bastard."

"I'll never think about it."

"What about Master Chief Hansel?"

"Yeah, he did too, but he was obvious."

"Rocko," Ares said, "it will be impossible to figure out who killed him."

"This isn't our call, unless he or they had seen us moving in."

"There will be an investigation."

"Police from outside."

"Probably, but they will be very careful about handling it. In fact, I agree with what Big has done."

"What was that?"

"Not burning those boxes."

"Ah."

Ares smiled. "Could this be an oasis?"

"A good one, Ares."

The name of Colonel de Mposi finally reached us. It was confirmed to us that the man was not on the campus.

The Mposi Master Chiefs were making attempts to calm things down and be conciliatory with the barrack residents. The attempts to play nice pops in front of us were equally unsuccessful and more publicly embarrassing when the real Master Chief Sánchez was coming out, little by little.

In mid-December, while many of the kids were under lockdown, the rain intensified, but Colonel de Mposi, as the most watchful figure in the campus, had begun the hard task of cross-examining and made a speech under the rain about finding the killers among us or bringing the authorities in to do so.

Hour after hour, day after day, rain or no rain, he would call kids, leaving us for the last.

That day, Ares and I had a serious conversation outside the barracks. We chose the big and flat tree several feet from the gorge, like an umbrella. We picked up Lagi, the waterboy, as a good source of gossip and information. A boy we could trust, who knew things.

"You had said this isn't our concern, Rocko."

"We went there, and we know a lot, Ares. We have their written reports, most importantly the ones from Mr. Mposi."

"This is going to explode."

"Not if we keep it under the radar. I think the killer knows us."

"Very well, Mr. Rockefeller, let's do it."

"Where can we find Lagi?"

"He's a resident of Barrack Number Four."

We went there, but Lagi was not at home. Cara Roja told us he could be at The Jungle Club, a place all teenagers of the Mposi campus visited and had a good time at.

"If you don't find him back there, he may be with Eel, dreaming of escaping."

Mel "Eel" Elinghton was in Barrack Number Three playing chess with Ronald "Egg" Eng. He was winning five-three, and we did not bother to ask him what he knew about Alejandro's death.

The Jungle Club was a little crowded, and none of those present was paying attention to us or the rumor of Alejandro Sánchez' death. The kids were playing frog jumping with wild berries and pecans as money, as well as getting scorpions to fight and pitting poison dart frogs against assassin bugs, wandering spiders against giant centipedes and bullet ants against centipedes in the Roman Arena of the Club.

We moved into a narrow path, and we needed to pay a fee. If you didn't have it, you could pay next time. The club belonged to Yu, who was partnered with Witz. We saw them sitting in the VIP Room with Rick and Col. We waved at them and nodded. They nodded back. We walked to a salon, where a ceiling of roots, trunks, branches and leaves had been built by the toughest kid in the barracks, who went by the name of Etmo "Witz" Markowitz—yes, Witz had designed the place, built the ceiling and the Roman Arena. He had the mind of his father, who was the head of the International Draft Firm. He had a unique talent. Somehow, there was a mystery surrounding him.

We found Lagi watching his precious wandering spider held dead under a dozen bullet ants.

"Hi Lagi."

"Hi Rocko. It's the first time I've seen you here. What's up?"

"Can we have a word with you?"

"You pay for a drink."

There were drinks in The Jungle Club and more.

We selected one of the rock sections, where it was a little quiet, away from the noises of a group of kids playing the Kiss Band.

We sat.

Marc "Tar" Tarrison brought some coconut water. If one kept coconut water for a week or so and combined it with sugarcane roots and beets, then one had a mix that was pure throaty alcohol, and they called it "A Teen" whiskey.

The drink arrived.

"Who pays for it?"

"Can we waive?"

"Not this one."

"All right, Rocko," Lagi said. "I'll pay it."

From his heavy coat, he produced a bag of seeds and paid for the drinks.

"What is going on, Lagi?"

He paid attention to us. First, he looked at Ares, and then at me.

"You are not going to play Master Chief with me, uh, Rocko?"

"No, Lagi."

"They saw Big carrying boxes out of that sick bastard's office."

This confirmed what I had told Ares and the others.

"And?"

"We know he did not act alone."

I saw him glancing in the direction of Witz and his entourage.

"Is there anything else?"

"What about?"

"The death of the Master Chief."

"Don't worry. Your circle elite did not kill him."

He drank.

We drank too.

"How are you sure?"

As he was about to reply, he saw that Witz was coming.

"Hello there."

Lagi knew what had happened to him the other day in the field, but what he was going to say was linked to Witz.

"Drink?"

"Sure," I said, indicating a seat.

"Ares, drink?"

"Why not, Witz."

"Hey, Tar."

"Got it, Witz."

"Can we have some privacy, Lagi?"

"Yeah. See you around, Rocko."

"Yeah, Lagi. Hey, thanks for the drinks."

Tar brought drinks.

Witz lifted his coconut glass and drank. He fell silent and he had across his face a dark expression, an expression that I was seeing for the first time. He surveyed the place, which was now a little quiet. The games and competitions among insects had ended and the kids were in groups, talking, thinking.

"I was ready to move to England for the second transformation of my life, and my acceptance at the University of Oxford made me see how important it was. I was happy, and I was so excited. I called Daddy and told him the news. I heard him cry, and that was cool, you know. Then, something happened upstairs, screams. I didn't mind what Mom had done, choosing a second way of living, but I understand what Dad had said. She had chosen wrongly, a man who constantly abused her."

The young Markowitz ran upstairs, hearing his mother calling for help, and he found her naked, covered with blood, with Karl Gavertolm beating her and cutting her with this long Japanese sword. He was drunk and, according to the High Court of Concord, New Hampshire, she, too, was drunk and on drugs. He pulled a chair and he didn't know how many times he raised it against Karl Gavertolm.

He stood over his mother, and he called his daddy.

"He still loved Mum, and he had to make a sacrifice. Many of our daddies do, to become the figure we love, but Mum had not seen it."

Chapter 46

Greta O'Donnell Newton, daughter of Lawrence and Rochelle O'Donnell Braddick, was a difficult woman and weak against temptation, and her family had traditional roots in New Hampshire and beyond. They were rich and established, handling the Architecture & Interior Design Company as a family entity until Otto Markowitz came along.

He brought something unique to the business, breaking the family monopoly of the O'Donnells.

His grandfather, David Deemer O'Donnell, a former Supreme Court judge who had retired the previous year and who was a critic of Otto Markowitz, told his son that as long as the Markowitz Firm maintained its presence in the New Hampshire Design Territory, his traditional name could never be the same.

"What is the answer?"

It was Greta.

Both sides saw the opportunity for conquest and victory. It was not a matter of stealing through deceit, intimidation and force, but rather by taking what lawfully belonged to Markowitz, but Etmo's birth changed Otto Markowitz' heart. He was a father now, and Greta had given him a son. It had helped accelerate between the young lovers a growing thirst for love, and Otto realized it was good for the young boy, approaching everything with a new hope.

David D. O'Donnell's death was followed by that of his son, after which Rochelle gave the wheel to Greta to continue the tradition of the O'Donnells. A drastic change had overtaken Greta. Otto's social manners had changed as well, with successive parties, drinks and drugs. Though she did not fully articulate it, Otto was the most bothersome man she had ever known.

The young Etmo, now a teen, smart but very conservative like his mother and quiet like his daddy, appeared to bring about a balance between the two.

That day, as on other days, Greta had enough, and with unabated aggression, brought up the desire to leave, and she left, taking the young Etmo with her.

"She lied to me twice."

Ares and I wouldn't dare give him a friendly reply, and we knew after that remembrance all would be alright, but there was more from Witz. The way his mum wanted him to pay for killing her old lover, knowing her son wanted to defend her.

"She accused me, but Daddy made this place a last resource."

Little by little, what he had behind those eyes came out. He touched his face, and he looked away. We saw on his right side the scar of a knife. We knew what had happened. They said he had cut himself in the sugarcane field.

"No?" I asked. "That's what we heard."

"He did it to me."

Ares' reaction was different from mine. He leaned backward. That information had first come from Lagi to Popo and then landed before us. I was curious.

"Are we talking about the same Master Chief Hansel?"

"No, Overseer Sánchez."

More surprises. Still. We were confused.

He drank from the coconut glass. He remained quiet for a minute or two.

"He raped me."

There it was. Alenjandro Sánchez was a pervert, a slippery sicko.

"How long?"

"Two years."

"And have you been waiting all that time?"

"I needed solid ground, and I was waiting. I was under Hansel's protection, and he knew. I needed them away from any suspicion."

"This couldn't be coincidence, could it?"

"No, Ares. I heard you guys want to escape. As you, Rocko, had done. I began to keep an eye on you guys."

"I can see you play with your luck, Witz."

"I fought with you because I didn't have any choice, Rocko. I was under them, and Alejandro was just waiting for you. But he noticed you were quite different from the other kids, and when he heard I was defeated, he began to look for another way. Hansel and him beat me all day along."

"Oh, bastard."

"Why didn't you come to us, Witz?"

"I was fucking embarrassed, Rocko."

"That was a teenage fight."

"Indeed. But they did not see it."

"Whatever you have been through, it's still me," I said, stretching my hand out to him.

"Sure?"

"Sure, Witz. I am with you, man."

He squeezed my hand. "It's true what the kids say."

"Bad things? I hope not."

"That you're a 100 percent teen."

"That's cool."

Ares stretched his hand out, and he said, "I'm with you."

"I appreciate it, Ares."

"What are you going to do?"

"I'm going to find Josh Hansel. I know he has something to do with the six kids missing."

"Be careful."

"I will."

Chapter 47

The next morning, there was a break from the rain and there was tremendous activity in Mposi—cleaning and preparation. Master Chief Guerra came to our barracks and took Sol to Colonel de Mposi in his office, where he was kind of sick.

He communicated to Al, who was below the ditch, and he communicated to Ares, who was walking in the plaza, cleaning the mud and broken trunks and trees.

We began to worry.

When the plaza was being cleaned, they moved to the other part of the Mposi, joining forces with M3 and M2. Right away, we had a problem with Master Chief Hansel of M3. His kids were to clean along the ravine and we, M1, were to pull the mud, leaves and other shit, but Josh Hansel had ordered the opposite. Master Chief Guerra was not among us, and Gil told Master Chief Sandhou what Mr. Guerra had said to us.

"Hey, just follow what Josh said."

"Well, no. I won't," Gil said. "We know what Master Chief Guerra has told us."

When Master Chief Hansel heard Gil refuse to jump into the ravine, he walked towards him, now surrounded by Ab, Popo and But, to repeat his message. The kids surveyed Hansel, and he reacted with some hesitation.

Some kids believed that the arrival of Master Chief Hansel inflamed the new situation I had created, leading to further escalation by a couple of kids who did not like him at all. Witz had broken away from his circle, and he didn't think about the potential damage Witz and other kids could cause to his reputation, given all the connections he had had with Alejandro Sánchez.

He glanced over at me, and I heard him speak with Ha, a kid who wanted to occupy Witz' place. "This kid is trouble. He must pay for it."

Ha, who was the fifth elite of the new group of and a former entourage runner in Witz' group, was not the only boy. There was Phil "Patel" Patterson, and both of them announced they would make Witz and others (me) scream.

There was an agreement between Ares, me and the kids to not cause any provocation. And there were promises from us to Witz.

Each group was intense.

Up on the plaza, Master Chief Guerra appeared. "Hey, Mr. Agdain, Mr. Mposi requests your presence in the office."

The last kid of M1 was me. The decision had been made for the next day. That day, it rained, and they made all of us clean the mess again.

Master Chief Guerra told me the meeting was still on and that he was going to see me at 10. From what I had heard, knowing that the kids had discovered what had been kept from them, such as letters and presents from their families, they focused on the death of Alejandro Sánchez.

I was prepared, and when I stepped into the Office of Colonel de Mposi, I knew half of his life. Dressed in a military-inspired regal jacket and loose pants, he sat behind the wooden desk. He still had that secret expression on his face, the seriousness of God, and that assumed arrogance. This man had a struggling soul and painful mind.

Ruth Canon de Mposi was born July 12, 1937, in Middlebury, Vermont. He graduated from MYAG University in 1957 and the University of Vermont Law School in 1962. He married his sweetheart, Yoland Tavt, and with her he had five children, due to which a nightmare had begun. All of them were girls until the last one, Roman. His children started to die before his eyes. One day, Lucy, after she had come back from school, ate and went to her room, where she killed herself, leaving a note with a question mark.

Mysteriously, Glenda would follow her a week later. There was speculation that it had to do with school or her peers, but there was no way to confirm the rumors. The same was the case with Heidi, Diana and Elaine.

By that time, Mr. Mposi was disappointed with life. While his love for his wife Jean was still strong, he went to fight the Niet Nan War, angry, disillusioned and wanting to die. They began to recognize him as a fearless fighter, a real American, a patriot, and they took him to fight other wars.

In 1977, Roman came into the world. A well-established American citizen, Roman gave Mr. Mposi more than hope, a new way of seeing himself as lucky, until tragedy struck him once more.

Roman was killed by a rich kid like us.

I could not yet establish the links between Mr. Mposi and the other fathers who had sought help from him, and I doubted that my father had called him to this place for me. Why I was here, I had no idea.

Mr. Mposi grasped his cigar. He did not light it. He looked at Master Chief Guerra and his assistant, Matle Sandhou.

His lover, not a regular office-keeper, Renita Borzaga, made her appearance, carrying coffee, and every evening she left Mposi to go back to her Indian village. She glanced at me, and she slid the mug onto the surface of the table.

"Some kids during the heavy evening rains broke into Mr. Sánchez' cottage, killed him and stole boxes he kept. The boxes I don't care much about, but his death is something else."

"What do you want from me, Mr. Mposi?"

"Any information you may have."

"What for, exactly?"

He pressed his eyes into mine. At this time, I challenged him openly.

"It's the law, Mr. Rockefeller. He's a human being."

I tried to hold back, but I could not.

"It seems you stake your reputation on what Alejandro Sánchez was before these missing kids, and care less about what happened to Jason Yadiro, Christopher Davie, DeVon Curtin, Ronald Eng, James Estavroock and Mel Elinghton."

I also mentioned a recent accusation made by one of the Mposi compound kids that Master Chief Sánchez linked Master Chief Hansel to the disappearances of other kids, causing several escapes and deaths.

"Enough."

"What? Didn't you know that?"

"I said enough!" he slammed his hand on the desk, sending each item flying. But my attempts to make him understand this isolated place, to get him to make a choice between good behavior and being a good citizen, fell flat.

I saw him getting up, but I didn't see what happened next. I felt his hand on my face, but I was on my feet. Anger seized me. Lifting a chair, I tossed it towards him. I missed. Mr. Sandhou held me. I fought with him.

"You dare hit me again, I will kill you. Heard me?"

Mr. Guerra pushed Mr. Sandhou away from me.

"You stay away from me. You take him out of here and increase his quota to 5,000."

"I am a Rockefeller! I have told you many times. None of you are going to break me."

"Then I want to use Canopy's Hole against you."

I shook my arm out of Mr. Guerra's grasp. I turned and came out of the office. Rain started to pour. I was very upset. This time, I wouldn't go anywhere. I would face all the odds.

In the barracks, Ares, Sol, Ab, Gil, Popo, Al and Big were waiting for me. They saw my face. Ares approached me. He stood next to me, and cool as he was, he did not dare to speak. Eyes brought a hot mug of chocolate.

"When you are ready to speak, we are here."

I was ready to speak, and I told them why I was upset, and I also told them about Canopy's Hole before I revealed the truth about Mr. Mposi, which I had read in the files we took from Mr. Sánchez's cottage.

Gil was the senior among us, having been there for two-and-a-half years. He told us about Canopy's Hole, which consisted of a rope and cage hanging from a tree.

"I saw him use it against Richard Archjen, and we called him Jen, and he was something."

"What happened to him?" Al asked.

"They found him dead. Snake poison."

"We're not allowing Rocko to meet the same fate."

"He wouldn't dare. I got him."

"He can do whatever he pleases, Rocko."

"Not anymore, Ab."

"We are with you, Rocko."

"I know."

Ares and I had a talk with Witz behind the cypress.

"I heard about what Mr. Mposi wanted to do."

"He won't." I nodded to Ares. "We found these, and they belonged to you. You take your time to read them, alone."

He took the small package from Ares. We saw his hands were trembling. He opened it, but he did not go further when he recognized the handwriting of his father.

"I will catch you guys later."

"Sure. Don't rush."

We fell silent. We watched the rain.

Ares spoke. "Are you going to go ahead with our next plan?"

"It's time those kids know the facts, Ares. Don't you think?"

"I do, and this will be a bomb."

"So be it."

"Mr. Rockefeller, may I have a word with you?"

We saw Mr. Guerra ambling down along the pathway across the muddy ground.

"What is it?"

"Alone?"

"Ares has become a brother to me, and he will stay."

"Very well. I persuaded Mr. Mposi not to send you to Canopy's Hole, not in this rainy season. There is a condition."

"I will not let that coward beat me. Hell no."

"You must tell us where those boxes are."

"I see, Mr. Guerra. You have become a delivery boy. Not that Black Shadow Man anymore."

"Don't judge me so quickly without knowing me, Mr. Rockefeller."

"Well, you tell your master, I won't tell him a thing. In fact, I have a present for him." I produced a letter from my pocket, a letter that was written to his wife Jean when Lucy died, accusing him of having given the teen girl inadequate attention. "I am more than a boy, Mr. Guerra."

"That is a mistake, young man."

"Is it, sir?"

Chapter 48

I was awakened by cold water. At first, I thought it might have fallen through a hole in the ceiling of the barracks. But as the sleep cleared from my head, I realized that I was suspended from giant branches and had nothing below me.

I screamed, "Get me out of here!"

I turned my head, and it was not day yet. It was dark, raining, and cold. I noted I was not alone. I felt the presence of people. I believed that the Mposi Master Chiefs were there. The new situation made it clear to me that this was certainly not the case and that there was only one Master Chief, who cared little about my pain or the fact that I was screaming.

Josh Hansel and his new runners, Patel and Ha, watched me from the firm ground with an expression of satisfaction.

I looked below.

"I changed it. It was supposed to be from a trunk, but I said I can do it better. Can you guess? There are more than 5,000 kilometers below you, solid rock, and eventually, I will rub this rope with wild honey. Next? There will come a hundred bullet aunts and they are going to make it a festival. See, Mr. Rockefeller? You're going to tell me where those boxes are, and of course who killed my brother-in-law, Alejandro Sánchez."

Fear. It made me laugh. "I can see it runs in the family."

That upset him. He started to swing the rope right and left. It made me feel like death was close, but I didn't yield.

"You're going to tell me."

"What I see is that your brother-in-law was a perverted and sick man."

"You have a big mouth, hear me?"

It was then that Colonel de Mposi appeared through the bushes.

"I got that information from Mr. Guerra."

"I was not aware I had said a thing to Mr. Guerra."

"I came here to tell you that your new Master Chief is Josh Hansel, and you have been transferred to Barrack Number Three."

"You think it's going to make me fragile."

"No one has remained for 30 days in that cage. You should drink as much water as you can now, because you will need it."

Ares asked Popo, "Where is Rocko?"

"That's what I wanted to ask you."

Ares walked to the end of the barracks and looked out at the place where I sometimes stood looking at the passage.

Gil, Ab, Sol, Al, Big and Eyes joined him.

"Maybe they took him."

"I won't be quiet."

"What are you going to do?"

"Speak with Master Chief."

"Yeah. He must know."

Master Chief walked purposely with his machete in hand, taking swipes at the green snakes that had erupted into the chicken house that had a dozen chickens, cutting them, holding them and tossing them below.

"Master Chief Guerra, may I have a word with you?"

"What is it, boys? Hey, kill that."

Ares jumped ahead, grasped the snake and shook it twice.

"A word, Master Chief."

"I am listening, Mr. Agdain."

"You must know where Rocko is."

"I believe he has escaped."

"Not this time, Master Chief."

"Well, I am no longer his Master Chief."

"What did you say, Master Chief?"

He looked at Popo. "He was transferred to M3."

"Since when?"

"I received the call from Mr. Mposi this morning."

"You know there is more to it than that."

"He isn't my responsibility."

"Was he before, Sire? Or was anyone for that matter, Master Chief?"

"I will ask Mr. Mposi."

"We want an answer today, sir."

"You will have your reply, Mr. Agdain."

Acting in a strange manner, Master Chief Guerra went to see Master Chief Hansel. He found the barracks empty and the hammocks wrapped up against the wall, except one that a mosquito net was still on. The morning sun penetrated the barracks through the door, revealing a person lying on the hammock.

Master Chief Guerra came over to the hammock and swept the mosquito net away. He saw Mr. Markowirtz crying and a couple of letters on his chest. He was unable to put them away, but Master Chief Guerra ignored them.

"Where can I find Mr. Hansel?"

Quickly, he dried his tears and put the letters in his pocket.

"He left very early, Master Chief."

"Hunting?"

"I don't think so. Patel and Ha are with him."

"Be careful, son."

He kicked the muddy terrain, strolling towards Mposi's office. He found Mposi arguing with Josh Hansel. "I want results, Josh."

"You will have them."

"Yeah, Guerra."

"Fuck off, Josh." To Mposi. "You promised you wouldn't put that kid in the hole. Where is he?"

Colonel de Mposi crossed his fists on the table. "I am sick and tired of you, Guerra."

"For what? I'm beginning to see what's happening."

"Damn you! We agreed about this. Their fathers have put them here for a reason, so that we feed them with the truth."

"I've had enough. These kids, Yadiro, Davie, Curtain, Eng, Estavrook and Elinghton, were not supposed to die. There is a limit."

"I see Mr. Guerra has been smelling weakness."

No one knew how Mr. Guerra reached him, and, with his left hand, sent him to the wall. Josh, bleeding and cursing, produced a pistol.

"Josh!"

"I will kill this Latino shit!"

"Put that away, Josh."

"Next time, you will be dead, I tell you."

"Hey, Josh. Go. Be sure to make him talk."

"After all, you put him in."

"One word and all of us are fried, Rudolph."

"Yeah."

"Where are you going?"

"Cool myself off."

"I need you and Matle to go to Turtlon Place and speak with Lemore."

"Now? In this rain?"

"It isn't raining. We want to be sure the news of the six kids stays here."

"Very well. But you tell Josh once again, he will lose the head."

"He isn't like you, Guerra."

Turtlon Place was a village about 70 kilometers from Mposi. It was like a depot—all correspondences for Mposi ended up there. The living souls settled there were Indians who had left their tribes and drifters from the mainland of Brazil, who would have 30 days to make the trip. A single bar and a series of saltbox houses, which they had built against the forest.

Rudolph Guerra's shoulders were marked. Not at this particular moment; rather, after the last conversation he had with me.

The English truck reached the limits of Turtlon Place and crossed the local bridge. Illuminated by the light of the torches a short, bearded man, dressed in heavy denim, waved to Matle Sandhou.

The truck stopped. Matle got out. Rudolph stepped out and saluted Ollie.

"As I said to Matle, I have some packages for Mposi. Come in." He entered and addressed himself to Guerra. "I got a bottle."

"Where is the package?"

Ollie Lemore was a mess. Boxes, packages, newspapers and equipment were everywhere. He knew how to find his things.

"Over here?"

"We have hours to return."

"That's fine."

"Any news from the six kids?"

"Everything is quiet."

"Help me here, Ru."

"I will bring the other package."

It was quickly brought, and Ollie found an old pistol. Mr. Guerra was expecting that action would take place outside the house, where there was less visibility. He was capable of getting Ollie with a single bullet. Mr. Sandhou did not lose his nerve at Guerra's prompt—he took the shot.

Mr. Guerra breathed a little, cursed Sandhou, Ollie, Mposi and everyone who was responsible for the bullet he had received. Deliberately, he began to prepare to take care of himself, but he realized that the bullet had reached deep inside his body.

"Ru, it's me. Don't shoot."

"*¿Qué hace aquí*, Renita?"

"I heard Ruth talking with Sandhou about this."

"You knew."

"Yes."

"Why didn't you tell me before?"

"I thought he was going to do it in the jungle. I guess I was wrong. C'mon. I will take you to a place and she will fix you."

"Then you know who I am."

"A little."

Chapter 49

It was still a rainy morning—cloudless, and the sun was directly on my cage. I hadn't eaten since the day before. I watched Patel and Ha sit on a trunk and toss me seeds from above, when I saw a procession of bullet ants marching along the rope, approaching the cage.

I could think of no reason why I was going to die young, suspended inside this balloon made up of fibers and away from a civilized world I still loved. I didn't expect to die, not now, down there and at the mercy of these ants.

I saw leaves moving and trees shaking.

"Hey, Patel."

"Shut up, Rocko. This is your lucky day."

"Why are you doing this?"

I turned, and I saw Ares, Gil and Popo, led by Witz.

"Bring him down, Patel."

"You are not part of us, Witz. I am the leader."

"I made you, remember?"

"You made a shit of me, but I am the leader."

"Hey, what is this? A seniority reunion."

"I am going to get him out of there, Master Chief," Ares said, moving away from the group.

"This is my call, Ares."

"Ah, you are going to face me?"

"Like a man."

"I am not in that circle\ of teenage bullshit." He produced his personal pistol.

Witz did not get down, and it seemed he had grown. "How does it look, a Master Chief confronting a teen with a pistol?"

"You boys don't get it. I will kill each of you and no one will give a shit."

"Yeah, you're right, but the kids who saw you are not afraid anymore."

Patel looked at him. "What is he talking about, Master Chief?"

"Nonsense!"

"He has to do with the deaths of six kids."

"Shut up, boy."

"And I was the one who killed that bastard brother-in-law of yours."

"You!"

Popo slipped left and a rocky projectile hit him. Josh Hansel lost balance, his fingers lost their grip on the pistol, and his head slammed into the ground. Witz did not have time. He leaped over him.

Patel and Ha, who were still loyal to their Master Chief, wanted to block Witz. Ares and Gil ran towards them. The boys collapsed to the ground. They began to throw and push each other. Popo stayed where I was.

Josh got to his feet, looked around, wanting to find his pistol, and he felt his body seize up. He turned and then found himself on the floor again. Witz began to punish him.

Patel stood upright, bullying Ares. Ares' right-left connected with Patel's face. It made him bleed from his lips.

Gil didn't take a chance with Ha. Using karate techniques, he took him down.

Meanwhile, Popo tried to do his best to bring the cage to the ground, but he couldn't because the second rope was entwined with the first and held it tightly along the edge of the cliff.

"It's hard to do this, Rocko."

"Don't let the rope loosen, please."

"I won't."

Now the damned bullet ants. I was thinking of them and about Witz. He was underneath Josh. He needed air. His efforts were petering out when Gil pulled Josh off him. Witz coughed and pushed further. Josh lost his balance once more, and the impact of Witz' push had sent him to the edge of the cliff. He held onto the root. Witz saw him and wanted to save him from falling. He was about to reach Josh's hand, working hard to bring him up, trying to catch his breath, but Josh fell.

Witz lay in place for a few minutes.

"I tried. You guys saw I tried."

Gil lifted him up.

"You did. You did."

"Hey, guys, I need help here."

With the help of Ares and Gil, Popo was able to figure out how Josh had made the knot, and carefully they pulled the cage to the muddy ground.

I firmly kicked the fiber wall and tossed myself into the mud because of the stings, but I was alive. Then I got to my feet. I saw that Patel and Ha were still bleeding.

"You tell me what I am going to do to you two."

"I am sorry, Rocko."

"Bring me that honey, Popo."

"No, please, Rocko."

I took the honey from the coconut mug and bathed them with it. I took Patel and forced him into the cage that had a thousand bullet ants. I saw him crying, urinating and begging me.

"Sometimes, you must choose a side, Patel."

He pushed him away from me, and without saying another word, I began to walk to Mposi. Ares, Popo, Gil and Witz followed me.

In the Mposi compound, at two p.m., we found all the kids of the barracks kneeling in the plaza, and Master Chiefs Ranjit Sandhou, Miguel Bojorguez and Dieng Chung pointing at them with long rifles.

So when Colonel de Mposi called me over, I saw that face—Joe Mendoza's face—and he was not alone. With him were Paul McCoy, Alfredo Izmatch, Guillermo Hurtado, Brian Habert and Yokata Metlow, an elite group under Colonel de Mposi, their bodies covered with weapons, and they were half a foot away from him.

I wasn't perturbed by them. I communicated with Ares and the others, and they understood that the second phase of Mposi's strategic plan had started to emerge. I had made a decision in the recent days to no longer be afraid of Colonel de Mposi. What I had read and what I had understood was that he wouldn't hurt us. On that count, I was wrong.

"I see you have survived, and you've come here to join us." He looked around. "I presume Master Chief Hansel won't join us."

"Unfortunately, he won't, Mr. Mposi."

"It's too bad. I had begun to like him."

"Me, too," I said ironically.

He stepped forward, his expression that of a father figure, his eyes on me. He said, "You have decided to keep your mouth sealed about what we discussed."

"That's the way to survive."

"Once more, where are those boxes?"

I thanked myself. I had removed the boxes from where Big had told us he put them. There was a reason. When we had begun to have doubts about the death of Alejandro, Ares, Gil, Popo, Ab and others, including me, had believed he had killed Mr. Sánchez. There was no other explanation. Then Lagi had come along and things had started to change. And when Ares and I heard Witz' confession, I decided to remove the boxes from the ravine and transported them to another place.

I knew there would be a little pain and suffering, but that would be good for everyone in the end, because that would be our passport to staying alive until we could find another way of getting out of here.

With his eyes on me, Colonel de Mposi approached our barrack, then scanned our faces. He examined Ares, Ab, Gil, Sol, Popo, Big, Al, Jet, Eyes, Witz (who changed places with Ab) and me. "I know each one of you belongs to the circle, and somehow one of you has to know. Do I make myself clear? Oh, yes. Bring him."

Joe Mendoza waved to Alfredo Izmatch and Yokata Metlow. They jumped over to Ab and grabbed hold of him. Ab fixed his eyes on Mr. Mposi. "You will get nothing from me, Mr. Colonel."

They took him to the middle of the plaza and held him flat against a wooden bed. They stripped him of his shirt.

Colonel de Mposi stepped back, and he watched him.

"Last chance."

I did not expect anything else. He raised his hand, and Ranjit Sandhou, brother of Matle, tossed his rifle over his shoulders. He walked to a cage that was covered, opened it and brought out a wildcat.

The kids paid attention. Many of them knew how aggressive wildcats were. I exchanged looks with Ares and the others. We began to think. We had heard what Colonel de Mposi was going to do. He said a name—"The Cat Howling." It was a form of Brazilian torture that was used, back in the 19th century, to punish rebel slaves.

"Are you crazy or something? That's illegal."

"Not in my territory."

"Do it."

Ranjit walked over to Ab. He placed the cat over Ab's back and then he squeezed the cat's neck and tail. Furiously, the cat fanned out his claws and painfully scratched Ab's back.

"Ah!" Ab cried, shaking on the wooden bed.

"What is the matter with you, sir?" Ares screamed out, wanting to get up. A gun a few feet from him held him in place.

"Ares, calm down."

"Can't you see that, Popo? That's insane."

"Hold up, man."

I tried to adapt my thoughts to this new situation. I had forgotten about Ab's suffering and pain, and only thought about the value that was inside these boxes. I had forgotten what I had read and what I had told them, everything. But Ab's life was in danger.

I did not want him to be tortured or to die. When he belonged to us, he knew the circumstances.

"Tell me, where are the boxes?"

"We burned them, you sick bastard."

"Give me him. He loves it."

I started to watch them, especially the individuals who had come with Joe Mendoza, and when I was wondering where Mr. Guerra and Mr. Sandhou were, I recognized this was more than I had expected.

Joe Mendoza's group, their costumes, their hats, the boots worn by the Brazilian police, were all meant to make us feel scared, guilty, criminal, some of us more than others. There was a way in which they acted: they belonged to Colonel de Mposi's game, a game of extortion. This place (the whole meaning of Mposi) was attached to the letters I had read, and from the letters he wrote to our fathers and mothers more than others.

Registered Mail

Mr. Ruth de Mposi

Driver Rain, Box 170

Turtlon Place

Arizona Rainforest, MP

Brasil

0430-100

Mrs. Helen Popovic

861 E Dragram

Tucson AZ 85705

USA

Re: Unpaid $70,000

Dear Mrs. Popovic:

Attempts to contact you and secure payment to the institution by Mposi Administration have been to no avail.

Consider this our formal demand for full and immediate payment of the outstanding balance. If your payment is not received within 10 days of this letter, we will begin litigation proceedings to send your son to court again.

It is our hope that you will provide an acceptable response to this demand in order for both of us to avoid additional costs.

Sincerely,

Mposi Administration

Enclosure: Letters from your son will be put on hold temporarily.

Henry Aldridge

600 MAIN ST

PO BOX 88881

SEATTLE WA 98104

USA

Mr. Ruth de Mposi

Administrator

Registered Mail

Mr. Ruth de Mposi

Driver Rain, Box 170

Turtlon Place

Arizona Rainforest, MP

Brasil

0430-100

Monday, July 05, (19..)

Re: $100,000

Dear Mposi,

When credit privileges were extended to your institution, we (his mother & father) had confidence in your ability and willingness to pay our obligations promptly.

We have received his letters and the reports of his improvement. We are so happy to hear that he is all right and learning.

Please, write to us about when we will be able to see him. His mother misses him.

Thanks

Henry

The Mposi Campus

Att: William Rockefeller

Driver Rain, Box 170

Turtlom Place

Arizona Rainforest, MP

Brasil

0430-100

New York, May 10 (19...)

8118 Straw West Street

Middletown, NY 10940

Dear Brother >> Why didn't you write to me? This is my 24th letter. Are you angry with me? Please, please, please, write to me.

Your sister

Chapter 50

They removed Popo from the wooden bed and tossed him next to Al and Ab. When we looked at Colonel de Mposi, who had been trying not to lose his temper behind his paternal mask, our heart rates accelerated, our breathing quickened and our muscles contracted as we wondered what would be next. We became acutely aware not only of what we were doing but also of what he might think he was doing.

But I had decided I'd try not to feel guilty while I watched Ab, Popo and Al lie there in pain. I heard kids crying and asking for whoever had stolen the boxes and killed Alejandro Sánchez to come out.

I was firm about what I felt. Ares, Gil, Big, Witz and others saw what I was doing was important. They also began to see Colonel de Mposi was not the man he seemed to be.

And so, for the first time in my life, I was fighting for something, for others. If this was justice, a teenager's redemption, a mother's boy who had begun to grow, well, so be it.

I looked Colonel de Mposi in the eye and asked as gently and open-heartedly as possible if he could tell me why the boxes were so important, the boxes about which all this time he had not cared. "It's a secret, a secret that if you reveal, the entire foundation of Mposi, including you, will be history."

I was talking about the place, the layers of his persona, the lies, which made the kids see no hope but to escape and to die. I began to mention names.

"Ray Gaerm."

"Shut up, boy!"

"Bernard Harrison."

"Shut up!"

"Alan Fong."

"Take him and I will make him see what he has done."

Yokata Metlow came to me, but I kicked him. I did not run. I was sure, cool, fighting for a right, a place, showing him that I had the wheel and he could not kill me or them.

I told him as much, laughing to express the feelings of a teenager who had discovered his dangerous scam. The kids were confused and scared, but Ares and my circle had begun to see more than a teen. They had begun to see a man.

I felt a hammer directly to my head.

I lost consciousness.

Chapter 51

Renita glanced at Mr. Guerra.

"Ru! Ru! Stay with me, hear me?"

"I will."

"Almost there. Hear me?"

When he said no, she asked if he knew where he was. When he said yes, she asked again, "A boat or a car?"

"A car."

She smiled.

An hour later, she was driving along a narrow inroad near a lake. The rain was still pouring, but Renita was able to see the figure across the inroad.

She stopped the car. Getting out, she said, "Help me, La."

"Who is he?"

"I don't know yet, except that he is a Master Chief of Mposi, and he kissed Matle Sandhou, brother of Ranji and Ollie."

"How did you know that?"

"They pay us to know that."

La Tanya Blanchard grasped Mr. Guerra's shoulders, pulled him out of the car, and then Renita took him by the waist.

"He lost consciousness again."

"He's a handsome brawny one."

"Really, La? You first need to bring him back to life, and then ask if he likes you."

"Yes, Mum."

They moved into a well-made cottage linked to the river. It was one of those cottage houses built over the water.

La Tanya examined him. "I can cure him, and that will take all night."

"You tell me what to do."

"Make soup."

"Soup?"

"Yes."

"For him?"

"No, silly. For me."

"He's awake."

"Where am I?"

"You're in a secure place with two women who want to ask you a lot of questions."

"I need to go back."

Mr. Guerra had the intention of getting up, but Renita held him down gently.

"You can't. You've been shot and my friend has fixed you."

"Hi. You'll take a week or so to be yourself again."

"Thank you."

"La Tanya Blanchard, and you can call me La."

He glanced at La Tanya, smiled, and turned next to Renita.

"We're together. Don't worry. We're mother and daughter."

"I belong to the International Office of Fraud. I am an officer and am after Mr. Mposi, who has deceived so many families, typically by claiming he is running the best sting in the world. Being an administrator, he claims to give new opportunities to these kids, which their parents believe. He works with judges, lawyers, counselors. Once the kids are in Mposi, he starts to exploit them for money."

"How long have you been involved with it?"

"Not long. A year, perhaps, after five kids disappeared."

"You've done a messy job."

"It takes time, and I was doing my job until Alejandro Sánchez was killed and the boxes were discovered. I didn't know how important he was until I realized he kept most of the information under lock and key. Did you know he is the brother-in-law of Hansel?"

"I am aware of that."

"So what are you two?"

"The Migliaro family. Mrs. Migliaro hired us to find her son, Frank. There was an arrangement between Judge Riss Proano and the main prosecutor of the District Attorney's Office of Alabama, Gerhard Sakane, to give him 40 years. Are you familiar with the case of Smith-Migliaro? So the two lawyers, one from the victim' side and the other from the accused's side, agreed to work with the Migliaro family. They would reduce the sentence to a minimum of five years, and he would be free two years from now. But there would be a fee." Renita walked to a room and came out with a file. "He sent it to Frank."

It was a perfect pamphlet of Mposi Campus—100 kids dressed in uniforms, smiling, and in the background the green acres of coffee fields.

"I was familiar with that condition."

"I presumed he had told them about the disappearance of the boy, but he was still collecting from the Migliaro family the $50,000 fee to keep their son safe, while sending them letters and reports telling them that Frank was alright. His father, Elliot, decided not to send any money and demanded to see Administrator Mposi. I believe he met him, killed him and threw him in the river."

Guerra was not familiar with this particular case, but he was sure that that was the method of Colonel de Mposi.

"You're still playing his lover."

"I have to, but he doesn't trust me."

"There is a boy by the name of William Rockefeller." He paused. "I began to play it cool with him, watching him, molding him for what I am thinking, but I saw that he was too reckless. He was able to face Mr. Mposi, and he did not fear him. I recognized that he was smart about what would come next."

"Do you believe he killed Mr. Sánchez?"

"No, I don't think so. He must know where the boxes are and who killed him."

"Can I trust him?"

"He doesn't trust anyone, and that is why he is so special."

"I will try. Meanwhile, you will stay here with La."

"One misstep, Renita, you will not come back alive from the compound, even though you appear to be part of his soul."

"I need to keep it that way."

Chapter 52

"You're a strong boy," Yokata Metlow said, whispering from behind me.

Dieng Chung approached Miguel Borjorguez on the opposite side, not speaking, watching me against the wall.

"I won't take it, Miguel. This isn't what I've signed up for. Torture."

"Be quiet, Dieng."

"What is it, Master Chief?" Colonel de Mposi asked, turning completely towards Dieng Chung, who appeared like he would not back up.

"Physical pain isn't on the menu, Mr. de Mposi. You know," he said, peering at me, holding on.

"I know what, Master Chief Chung?"

The Master Chief did not hold back, and he said, looking straight into Colonel de Mposi's eyes without fear, "It isn't acceptable. I won't put myself to that task."

"You won't?"

"No, Mr. de Mposi."

"Where are you going?"

"I am done here."

"Hell no."

He saw de Mposi's handgun. "Are you going to shoot me?"

He pressed the trigger. "Is there any doubt?"

Miguel Bojorquez looked at Ranjit Sandhou, but Ranjit had already crossed the space of Joe Mendoza and his elites and stopped. Miguel felt alone in the middle of the room. He glanced at Me. Mendoza, then at Mr. de Mposi.

"I see you're by yourself, Master Chief," Joe said ironically.

"Very well, Mr. de Mposi, I am. So, what is the matter here?"

"Good," he replied, tossing to him the whip. "Each one of us is dependent on him. He knows where the boxes are, and that is all I want."

He grasped the whip, but he didn't move.

Chapter 53

At this moment, everyone was confused and scared. I was not alone in this room. Master Chief Bojorquez was here, and after he had hit my back with the whip (he didn't have a choice; Master Chief Chung had died for what he had believed in) he tried to convince me to speak.

"You fool. Tell them what they want. I promise you will no longer be punished."

I did not like this approach of his. His intention was weak.

"You coward."

During what followed, I did not pity him. Ares and Eyes were able to storm into the room, and they knocked him cold to the floor.

"Is he dead?"

"I don't know, Eyes. I don't care. Go, go and help Rocko."

Eyes came to me. "Once again, I need to take care of you, bro."

"I'm happy you will."

Ares took the weapons of Miguel Bojorques. "We'll need them." He approached and helped Eyes, holding me now, and both of them pulled me off the wall.

"We want to take you out of here."

"Where?"

"The club."

"Club?"

"Yes. Witz told us he built a second layer."

"He did, didn't he?"

"Yes. Popo, Al and Ab are there. Jet is curing them. How is the pain?"

"It's like a million bullet ants at once."

"You did good, Rocko. All the kids are with you."

"It isn't done, Ares. He killed Dieng."

"Who?"

"Colonel de Mposi. He refused to be part of this madness, and, as he was about to leave the room, he called him and killed him."

"We need to find help."

"We will, Eyes."

Below the Roman Club, again, I saw Witz' talent and promising mind. He greeted me with a hug, careful not to touch my back, which was on fire.

"Put him here, Witz," said Sol, who had become a great help. "I will cure that back, Rocko, and this is going to hurt."

"What is this?"

"It's the poison from the blue frog, and it is going to heal you."

I peeped at Popo, Al and Ab, and they nodded, telling me it had been working. I surrendered myself to Sol, who had studied medicine for a year as an intern.

Later, they fed me roots and wild meat and gave me water. A moment later, I closed my eyes.

We heard the voice of Joe Mendoza and his elites from the plaza, demanding to know where Popo, Al, Ab and I were, not leaving a single place unchecked. We heard Quillermo Hurtado and Ranjit Sandhou walk around the club, and then silence.

They found Colonel de Mposi standing at the crossing of the ditch, watching the place. He said, "We need to find him."

"They can't move fast. He is wounded, and so are the other kids."

"I don't care what you do, I need you to find him." He addressed Miguel, whose head was wrapped in bandages. "Bring me Ares and Witz."

"Yes, sir."

As he was about to move, he stopped, for the Indian Brazilian Renita Borzaga had appeared.

"I am here, Ruth."

He smiled and he waved to Miguel. When Miguel started walking away, he rubbed his hand over her face.

"I missed you."

"You gave me permission to see my daughter, didn't you?"

"Yes, I did."

He moved behind her into the office, pulled her over to him.

"I don't like to do this thing that is beyond any human morals. This rule, our rule cannot be broken."

"Motle isn't here."

"Where is he?"

"I sent him to Turtlon Place to take care of some business with Rudolph." He tried once more to pull her to him.

Renita pushed him off. Astonished and a bit embarrassed at having had his desire rejected, he asked her what was going on. But then Ranjit led Witz and Ares into the office and Colonel de Mposi's face changed. Miguel was not a fool. He saw Renita's body language. She was acting once more like an office keeper and cook. Mr. de Mposi appreciated it.

"Bring me a glass of rum."

"Sit, boys."

At this moment, Joe entered the office. He did not salute Miguel. He moved across the room and stopped near the table where the bottles of liquor were. He poured a homemade drink into a glass. He looked from that position at Renita and slid a glass of rum before Colonel de Mposi.

Mr. Mposi reached out for a cigar.

"I recently realized, as an administrator, that things in Mposi have got a little out hand."

Ares and Witz kept their eyes on him.

I told them about Ruth Canon de Mposi's family, his daughters, his wife, and then the boy by the name of Roman, and his death, and what happened next. He did not have anyone.

Except this place.

"We learned from our mistakes, as you will, too." He drank. His eyes were clean, lovely, a papa's eyes when speaking with his two teenage sons. "Every child's education includes learning how to deal with mistakes or hard choices, so he or she won't be locked up or hurt or even killed in a place you have never heard of before. The 'Cueva' Prison. The 'Black Worm' village and other places where I know none of you can survive. Despite my way of dealing with this situation, I built this place for the sake of self-learning, self-education, self-driving, self-understanding, making it by your own choices, and I am so proud I made you aware of your own capacity as a teen, a man, and finally an individual capable of acting alone in this society. Well, forget what happened today. I've decided to hand you your freedom."

Ares and Witz could not figure out what Colonel de Mposi's intention was.

He pulled out from the drawer two files with the names of Aram Agdain and Etmo Markowitz. The young teenagers glanced at the files and then peeped into them.

Miguel Bojorquez was tense.

Joe Mendoza was calm. Discreetly, Renita's eyes could be seen through a tiny hole.

"Just like that, Mr. de Mposi."

"Just like that, Mr. Agdain."

"The others?"

"They need to meet the requirements of Mposi's policy."

"It's too easy."

"Then, Mr. Agdain, I can send you back to court and add more years based on what you did to Master Chief along with Mr. Markowitz."

Ares raised one of his eyebrows superciliously. "It's funny how adults sometimes behave before us, and it appears they do not realize we are as smart as they are. In this case, Mr. de Mposi, you are that reflection of blankness."

"What was that, young man?"

"You cannot understand what these kids were thinking about you. It will be impossible. Your dead son Roman and your daughters would not allow it."

With tremendous force, he swept everything before him, but that did not make Ares and Witz jump; instead, they were still seated, staring at the furious face of Mr. de Mposi.

"You think your teen attitude will bring me down, mentioning my kids, and treating it as a joke. Well, you have picked the wrong daddy. Joe, put them in the plaza."

"You're not going to get anything good from us like that, Mr. de Mposi."

"We'll see."

I took some pork from Sol.

"It's about me, Sol."

"No, Rocko. It's about all of us. He is so desperate."

"We need to send someone to the nearby town, Sol. Perhaps we should communicate with the authorities."

"Don't trust them, most of them are close to Mposi."

I was silent. Then I asked, "Have they tortured them?"

"No, but Gil was unable to give them water or sweets. We expect to do so at night."

"It's dangerous to leave Ares and Witz there overnight."

"What do you suggest, Rocko?"

"How long should I stay down here?"

"Your back hasn't healed yet."

"How long will it take?"

"Five more weeks."

"That's too long."

"I am doing my best to prevent infection."

I looked over at Popo, who was sleeping like a babe. Al and Ab nodded.

"We need to bring them here, and to keep them until Mr. Guerra arrives."

"You still trust that bastard."

"I've seen his eyes, and he was a kind of mystery, but there is more of him."

"We will follow you, and the kids are ready to fight back. Many of them have been reading their fathers' letters and they have begun to open their eyes. I haven't seen Jet and Eyes cry so much. All in all, this has made them see."

"Somehow, they knew, and they understood that there was something wrong about this place. I am happy, thrilled even, by the scale of my discovery, but I don't want to see them hurt unless we have a solid way of beating him. After all, he has an army, and he can kill all of us."

"We are ready."

"Let me think."

"Can I explore the possibility of sending someone across the river?"

"We can drive the truck through the cave. I will wait two days, but you must seek a way to bring Ares and Witz here from the plaza."

Carrying a large tray, Renita served the table. Mr. de Mposi was seated, as were Joe, Paul, Alfredo, Guillermo, Brian and Yokata. To the side were Miguel and Ranjit.

Doing her job well, she slid onto the surface of the table, into his left hand, the glass of sugarcane juice.

"There is more bread."

"It's enough," de Mposi replied.

"Do I serve the others, Lazzon and Belen?"

"You're not serving them," Mr. de Mposi said. "They will soon be released."

"I will feed Mr. Guerra's chickens."

"What happened to him and Matle?" Brian asked, eating.

"They're taking care of some business in Turtlon Place."

"I have to go now." Casting her eyes down, Renita left the room.

Outside the dinner room, Renita walked away from the kitchen. She took a .38 caliber revolver out from under the oven and put it away, behind her back.

She came down to where the series of cottages were. She glanced in the direction of Mr. Guerra's cottage, and then moved quickly to Alejandro's place. She found nothing there.

Having another task to do, she ambled to the edge of the Mposi Campus, moving towards the plaza. She did not find Ares or Witz. Instead, Lazzon and Belen were tied up against the poles.

She backed up. She looked at Barrack Number One. She met a couple of kids who looked at her curiously. She entered the barracks. A few of them were lying on the hammocks. She found Sol cooking meals outside the barrack.

"You're in the wrong paradise, lady," Sol said, trying to imitate Renita's Indian dialect.

"I can speak English."

Sol paid attention to her.

"Yes. You can."

"I am a good woman, Sol. I am."

"Mr. de Mposi will do all he can to find those boxes. He did it to me, and you can see I have become another victim."

She produced a note and gave it to him.

"You will see I am different."

"Are you guys trying to play games with me? Well, you will have them."

"This is for Mr. de Mposi. I have to go. Please, give it to him."

After she touched his face, Renita ran to the other side of the plaza.

Sol dashed back to the left before running around the barracks, and he heard the sound of projectiles and Joe Mendoza yelling after he reached the trail to the plaza, and a voice shouting, "We see who has the balls here!"

Fear gripped the kids, and they started running everywhere.

"What is this?"

Sol went on this way until I decided to run away from the elites. I saw a couple of kids from Barrack Number Two running in front of him, heading to the forest. The cries of the kids were mixed with the sounds of bullets. As part of this, Sol and I were scared as well and were running with the residents, as the elites chased them down to the limits of the forest, screaming, "Stop! We'll shoot you!"

Yokata Metlow, another of Joe's elite men and Brian and Alfredo held a dozen kids at rifle point. They commanded them to walk before them.

Sol waited behind the bushes, looking across the compound on his way to the club. When he saw it was safe to approach the club, he did.

He bent over towards the ground and called out, "It's me!"

The heavy wall of rock opened.

He stepped in, and he looked at me.

"What's happening out there, Sol?"

"They're shooting them, Rocko."

"Shooting? With weapons?"

"Yes, Ab. Their rifles."

Ares and Witz got to their feet, as did Popo, Gil and Al.

We were in the inner space, and I said, "Where were Big, Eyes and Jet?"

"They went to explore the possibility of getting to the other side of the river."

"We are no longer safe here, guys."

"Ah, Rocko, I almost forgot."

"What is it?"

"Renita, remember her?"

"Yeah."

"She went to the barracks to see you, and she told me to give it to you."

"I don't understand." I grasped the note and read it.

"What does it say, Rocko?" Ares asked.

I peeped at him. "Mr. Guerra was shot at Turtlon Place. He is alive. Renita overheard it from Mr. de Mposi." I handed him the note.

"But who is she?"

"The big question is, what kind of role she is playing with Colonel de Mposi?"

"Or Mr. Guerra."

"I will meet her."

We heard footsteps above us.

"Ssh."

Then voices, which belonged to Quillermo and Paul.

"There is nothing."

"We need to find them, Quillermo."

I indicated the exit to them, and I led them out into the muddy ground. I told them we could take refuge in the sugarcane field. As I said this, we heard whispering—*"Hey, hey, Rocko, here!"* We turned our necks towards the sound and found Big, Jet, Eyes and But waving at us.

Crossing the terrain, we found a dozen kids, and they were wounded.

"Where have you taken them?"

"Trast here, he says there is a cave several miles off the river. We can move in and call for help, Rocko."

"Let us do it."

There was no work after that. I threw Trast over my shoulders and crossed the field. I did not know where he had been shot, and quickly, I felt blood all over my back.

Ares, Popo, Sol, Gil, Al and Ab followed me.

We kept moving.

I switched Trast to another shoulder.

"It must be around here, Rocko. Watch for the giant sequoia tree."

"Hey, watch out for a giant sequoia."

"It may be that babe, Rocko."

"That's it."

The giant sequoia had a hole in the middle of its belly, providing access to the other side of the rainforest.

"Where did you find this wolf, Trast?"

"You guys didn't know him. His name was Frank Migliaro, and we called him Fran. He discovered this place. We were ready to escape, but Gart, War and Fran were caught. I haven't seen them since."

"I'm going to put you on your feet, Trast."

"I can manage, Rocko."

"You have a lot of medical work to do, Sol."

"I need to examine each one of them."

I scanned the place, and it was indeed a cave, and I found insignificant insects or rodents here and there inside it. Ares was ready to catch them.

"Hey, guys, I found this."

"Do you know anything about this?"

"Fran and I collected things for our journal."

"No, this is a box."

"Open it, Al."

He opened it. Inside the box were documents, handwritten leaves that served as files of names, names like Rudolph Guerra and other Master Chiefs, the name of Colonel de Mposi, and what Frank "Fran" Migliaro had been fearing about the place.

"He knew."

"Yes. He was like you, Rocko. Reckless but smart."

"Well, let's settle in, and let Sol do miracles."

"Are we expecting any one of them to die?"

"Jeez, Eyes," Sol replied. "Let us be positive."

"Sorry. My bad."

"What do you need from us, Sol?"

"Fire, water, leaves and a strong will."

"Any idea, Trast?"

"We may have those things," he said, trying hard not to faint. "Go to that corner and count eleven steps backward. Under your right foot, you dig."

Ares did, and he began to dig. He retrieved a container that was given only to the Master Chiefs in the sugarcane fields. In it were a pair of knives, a machete, a flashlight, cocoa seeds and a map. There was also dried food but it was good. Sol saw a pairs of scissors and other medical tools, and he wondered for a moment.

"Was he a medical student?"

"Yes," Trast said weakly.

"Alright, let us do it."

We became one in the effort to make it smooth, collecting leaves for the bed, water and wild roots, careful about predators. The cave had become a teenage hospital, and the kids—Dan "Trast" Transbarger, Mario "Ben" Benquechea, Freddy "Kull" Kullohan, Peter "Mor" Moran, Jimmy "Hur" Hurwuzzon, Robin "Ro" Smirty, Earl "Chet" Chettonous, Daphne "Daphy" Eeny, Robert "Bob" Becerra, Edwin "Coye" Coyetton, Alvin "Alvin" Strongs, Nick "El" Beltran and Raymond "Ray" McMeas—had never seen such mutual encouragement and friendship before.

We were afraid for Daphy, Mor and Trast, who had been bleeding lots.

Again, Sol emerged a pro.

"Where do you think you're going, Mr. Guerra?"

"I can't be here, La. I need to go."

"Renita has said otherwise. Besides, you aren't strong enough."

"I must go and find a way to get help."

"I was beginning to like you, Mr. Guerra."

"I'm sorry for disappointing you."

"Yeah. Well, I'm going with you."

"Is that Renita's plan?"

"It is now."

"Do you have a communicator?"

"Oh, yes."

Renita moved to the right and watched the stones. She lifted one, and the opposite wall opened. She brought out a military bag and took out of it a satellite phone and a pair of pistols.

"You will also have this."

"How can I communicate?"

"Just press one, Mr. Guerra."

He did it and sat on the bed.

"Identification, please?"

"614 PGA Mosquito."

"How can I help you?"

"Amelia, please."

"One moment."

Pause.

"You're too early."

"He knows. He ordered me to be killed."

"We are on our way."

He disconnected.

"You're important."

"I was supposed to wrap it up like a perfect catch."

"You will, Mr. Guerra. Mum is working on it."

He winced at her.

"Mum?"

"Yes, she is my mum."

"How old are you, Miss La?"

She smirked. "I am old enough to be your sister. Well. Should we go?"

Chapter 54

When Ares, Popo, Witz and I reached Mposi, we perceived the place was isolated, and the kids who had not had a chance to escape were locked inside the barracks. We saw Colonel de Mposi's men guarding every corner of the plaza. Some of them were patrolling the area in front of de Mposi's office, and occasionally Joe or he would come out and survey the territory from the top of the slope.

"How are you going to meet her, Rocko?" Ares asked.

I tilted my head. The sky was stuffed with black clouds, and while the rain had stopped before we had reached the plaza, it was not done yet.

"The night will be darker. She has a habit of cooking for him, and I will take my time to meet her in the kitchen."

"It's a risky call, but it will work," Witz observed.

Popo had an idea. "Let us knock these guards out. They will not expect our presence."

"That's suicide, Popo," Ares said.

"Yes, I guess it is. I have started to hate those dudes."

We moved to the left, where there were a lot of bushlands that we could disappear into if we needed to run. From this side, the office of Colonel de Mposi was angled towards the series of cottages that belonged to the Master Chiefs. I told Popo to watch the right, Ares the center, Witz below where Barrack Number Three linked to the forest or within earshot of the voices that came from the barracks.

I recognized the face of Paul McCoy, the gray-headed, freckle-faced man yelling across Barrack Number Three to the kids inside, "Shut up, dirty maggots!" And even if they had tried to escape by breaking the wall made up of wood, it might have been impossible for them to get to the forest fast enough. They had promised them they would kill them if they tried to escape.

We heard the voices of the kids reach us once again. Each one of us recognized the voices of Patel and Lagi, who were part of Witz' entourage. Not to mention the voices of the barracks residents.

It seemed Paul McCoy had had enough.

"I go in," he said into a walkie-talkie to someone who was on the other side.

At this moment, Ranjit Sandhou appeared on the trail.

"Hey, let them scream."

"You don't belong to us, Master Chief of Shit. If your brother had done his job right, we wouldn't be in this mess, would we?"

"Whatever."

He moved in, and there was more yelling and screaming. As Paul was pulling Patel out, he started to beat him. He fell to the floor. We saw Witz's face change.

At this moment, Lagi, Yu and Ha came out.

"Get back! Go in."

We all watched them, and an observer could have read on our faces what we felt.

"Rocko, I can't hold on to it. "

"You should, Witz. See? We've a plan."

"That animal is going to kill him, man."

"All right." To Ares: "Can you distract Ranjit?"

"I will."

"Go."

"What about me, Rocko?"

"Watch our ass, Popo."

"Oh, I've become a brothersitter now, uh?"

I peeked at Witz. "You watch my back. Let's go."

"I'm carrying a pistol, Rocko."

"I know you are, but we need to play it cool."

Ranjit had turned, seeing a kid running below, and he began to chase him.

I tossed myself down below, and there was no one who could stop me. By the time I jogged across the mud, I was already on top of Paul and held him against the ground. Not expecting that surprise, he lost momentum,

"I told you about Rocko, Patel. There were no bad feelings from him, it was just a misunderstanding."

But Paul was still aggressive, so Ha put him to sleep, hitting him on his head with a stone.

"Where did you come from?"

"From the woods," I said, making it work. I made signals to Popo.

What?

Take them to the security place.

Okay.

"Bring all these kids and follow Popo."

"Where is he taking us?"

"To a safe place, Patel."

"Alright."

He moved into the barracks, and immediately he reappeared, leading more than 30 kids out.

"Are the other kids in the other barracks?"

"Yes."

"Let's take them one by one."

I communicated with the kids with my hands, telling them to move below the plaza, where they would find Popo waiting for them. They moved on, and so far it was good.

"I will stay with you, Rocko."

"I need you with them, and to help Ares, Witz and me make them pay."

"I can do it."

"You, too, Lagi."

He walked to where Paul was, still knocked out.

"I will tie him up inside."

From the main office came the call for dinner. I communicated with Witz and Ares, who was breathlessly running to us.

"What?"

"He may be looking for me down the ravine."

"She is calling for dinner. We will have a couple of hours to let the kids out of the barracks."

"We can do that, Rocko. You focus on Renita."

"All right."

I remembered the site of the hidden place. I checked, and I saw all the boxes were safe. I walked to Mr. Sánchez' cottage.

As I perused the place, it didn't take long for me to realize the elites of Colonel de Mposi were moving to the dining room. So I gradually made my way to the back of the cottage while I watched the movement of the barracks kids, led by Witz and Ares to the forest a few feet below the terrain. If I was going to make it, I thought at least the kids would be safe and I was hoping Gil and Al would find each other on the other side of the river.

I let myself into the cottage. Insects and snakes had begun to treat it like a hunting ground.

Finally, the last kids came out of the barrack. Rain began to fall. Darkness reached Mposi. I could hear conversation in the office, and I recognized that Renita had made her way out of the room and walked to the kitchen below.

I waited.

She disappeared into the kitchen.

I stepped carefully out of the cottage. I felt the rain on my body. At the outdoor bathroom site, I surveyed my surroundings.

Seeing nothing suspicious, I walked on, and I found her collecting some food.

"You were looking for me."

She turned and smiled at me. "Yes, I was. But not here." I saw her retrieve a handgun from underneath the oven. She picked up a heavy coat from a chair and put it on. She examined me. She went to a box that was on the floor and opened it. She took from it a raincoat. "This is better."

"Who are you?"

Smiling at me again, she walked to the rear door. "Put it on. Come."

Outside the kitchen, the rain had intensified. I followed her as she headed to Mr. Guerra's cottage, a little separate from the others.

Inside, she did not remove her coat.

"If you want to know, my real name is Melanie Leyva and I am here on a mission, William."

"I am listening."

"I am not alone and several miles from here, I have a place and my daughter. She is the same age as you. Her name is Sue."

I was aware there was more. I had seen her in the office serving Colonel de Mposi. Now, she was active, and her voice was strong, not a woman under anyone's command.

She might have seen the expression on my face. She had talked to Colonel de Mposi and she was aware of my presence. Finally, she told me about Mr. Guerra, and how she had saved him at Turtlon Place. Still, I kept wondering.

"We the kids have something that belongs to him."

"I know, William, and I can see you don't trust me."

"To be honest, I do not know, ma'am."

"Perhaps, among your peers, you have heard of Frank Migliaro. They have been calling him Fran. I am here because of him, but after a conversation with Rudolph, who has watched the problems unfolding here, they have become my problems as well."

"You might have heard Frank's name before."

Serenely, she produced a satellite phone from her coat. "Mr. Guerra was right about your perception, William. He has not misunderstood that." She held the phone to her ear.

"It's me. Put Mr. Guerra on the phone. Say what? I gave you instructions. Never mind. Put him on."

"What is it now, ma'am?"

"Mr. Guerra ... No. He's alright. He's here with me."

She handed me the phone.

With hesitation, I took it from her.

"Everything she has said is true, Mr. Rockefeller."

"You knew it from day one."

"Yes."

"How can I trust you, Master Chief?"

"It's a long history, Mr. Rockefeller, and very complicated to follow. But you must trust her and me."

"I need more than that, Master Chief."

"You're in my cottage, are you not?"

"Yes."

"Go the second room and face the window. There are two panels. Pull the second one up and down, and you will find the real Master Chief Guerra."

I took a moment to contemplate this. Renita did not speak. I moved to the second room and followed the instructions. There was a plastic bag, and inside it were the credentials of Mr. Guerra—Steven McGowan, of the U.S. Department of Justice Office of International Affairs.

I glanced at Renita, and slowly, I said, "I found it, Master Chief McGown."

"Keep calling me Master Chief. Soon, I'll reach Mposi. Can you put Ms. Leyva on the phone again?"

"He wants to speak with you."

"Thanks, William." On the phone: "Yes, I understand. Do you have any idea when they will land here?

"I'm not sure. But the call has been made and everyone is on the move."

"I will wait."

She put away the satellite phone just as they stormed in. Joe Mendoza and his killers spread themselves out in the room. Colonel Ruth Canon de Mposi strolled in. Calmly, he looked at Renita. "Do you think the colonel title was bought in a supermarket of Dan Nang? No, Miss Melanie Leyva. Hell no! I was owed it because I am a smart patriot."

"How did you know?"

"I've eyes everywhere. Believe me, you almost fooled me. In fact, you saved me. Guerra and you have been working together."

Renita breathed. "Ah, you still don't know."

"Is this a funny thing?"

"Perhaps."

I was doing all I could to hold onto the credentials of Mr. Guerra, but I had the cold eyes of Joe Mendoza on me.

Colonel de Mposi approached her and was not prepared for her quick response—as he was about to slap her, he found himself pushed back by Renita's left-left. She saw he was vulnerable, as Yokata was walking to me.

"He's mine, Yokata."

Paul McCoy crossed the room. Colonel de Mposi slapped Renita. She had seen Paul McCoy pressing his handgun directly to my head.

"Be careful, Paul. I need him to be alive."

"He and others beat me."

"I really don't care." He pushed him away from me, saw the window's panel. "Brai, search that window, and you, Ranjit and Miguel find out what he had hidden."

They found more items inside the panel of the window: pistols, money, Brazilian, Canadian and American passports and a communicator. There was a detailed report about what was happening in Mposi. Alfredo gave all of it to Mr. de Mposi. He showed no emotion or weakness.

"After all, you don't belong to him."

"It's over, Mr. de Mposi."

"I don't get it. Who are you, really?"

"I am working for the Migliaro family."

He stared at her for a long time and, remarkably, he remembered. "Ah, the Migliaros. I do believe the little fellow Fran killed himself, and I reported it to the authorities."

"The way you and Matle killed his father, Elliot."

"You have begun to annoy me, my dear Renita."

"It's over."

Suddenly, he screamed. "It isn't over, understand? It's over when I say so, hear me?" Then he fixed his long coat. "Now, you are going to tell me where these boxes are. This young man over here, Mr. Rockefeller, was taken from Sánchez' cottage."

"She doesn't know. She told you, it's over."

"I chose this place for a reason. No one has escaped from here. Eventually, they all will die in the rainforest. I think you have already experienced that."

"You're a bad man, and again, I get the feeling Roman had seen that."

"Don't, boy! He was better than any of you."

I had made him change his body language. I heard his words and brutal detachment. He spewed out his feelings towards the kids of barracks with contempt. He categorized us as nothing—mostly, it seemed, because of his past and his way of making up his own world after the tragedy that struck his family (most importantly, his children).

"I said before, they are watching you, monster."

"SHUT UP!"

His right hand went to the left and touched a pistol.

Renita, who had paid attention to what I had said and his movements, kicked Guillermo. I knew what would come next—and it came very fast. She targeted Mr. de Mposi.

"Be careful! She has a handgun!"

"Run, William!"

I heard bullets. Ranjit Sandhou wanted to protect Colonel de Mposi, and a bullet caught him, Guillermo and Miguel.

I pushed Brian Habert, who was pointing at Renita, and he crashed against the furniture. Yokata Metlow wanted to hold me, but I went through the window. I heard more shots, and Renita, whose humble skills had become lethal, was close to me.

"Keep running, William!"

I did.

"This way, Renita!"

"I am sure there is an abyss if we move that way."

"Now, it's time you trusted me."

"Very well."

"Stay close to me."

She did.

I found the trail despite the rain and then the narrow pathway to the cave.

"I never thought about this trail."

"Now I can trust you."

"Thanks."

I ran now with confidence. Several yards from the compound, I followed the path that Trast had indicated. A few minutes later, I saw the gigantic sequoia, which appeared even more magnificent in the storm.

After Trast was done telling Renita all he knew about Fran, we saw tears in Renita's eyes. She kissed him and noticed Sol's well-done job.

She gazed at me. "You have to be proud of what you have done, William."

"Without them, we wouldn't have made it."

"But you did, William by holding those documents."

"He's still back there." I had begun to hear the sound of rings.

Renita took out the satellite phone from one of her coat pockets.

"Leyva. Oh, yes. Where are you? I know the place." To me: "Mr. Guerra and my daughter are here."

Mr. Guerra confirmed all that Renita had told me—that he was shot and he had to kill Master Chief Matle Sandhou and the man by the name of Ollie, but he spoke with esteem about Renita's intention, to save him and her daughter, Sue. I recognized she was older than us, with the exception of Ares, who was already 19.

We were inside a temporary tent. Renita "Melanie Leyva" Borzaga" and Rudolph "Steven McGowan" Guerra had a conversation about how it was going to play out.

Sue brought a container filled with coffee.

"Have something. It's hot. You can use the lid."

She brought *beijinho*, a kind of coconut deserve, and *pamonha*.

"Thanks."

"You have to share. I didn't bring much."

"It will do," Ares said, pressing his lovely eyes into hers.

"Yeah."

Renita and Rudolph glanced at us.

"They will be here before sunset."

Chapter 55

The next morning, we were awakened by the sounds of helicopters and projectiles, and I could hear former Master Chief Guerra calling Renita, but she and her daughter were on their feet.

"They are here, but I see they did not follow the protocol to move in on foot."

"It doesn't matter."

"You stay."

"With all due respect," Popo said, showing him a pistol, "we came here to kick butts."

"No, you did not."

"We did."

We stepped ahead, and Master Chief glanced at Renita when he saw we were not backing down. "Is this your idea? This isn't a Boy Scout District, you know?"

Popo spoke. "As a matter of fact, I was a Boy Scout, and a good one."

He was followed by Ab, who mentioned a rich club that had trained him to be a good rich citizen, and then Witz and Ares. Me—I could not say I was a Boy Scout or anything, except that I was going with or without them. We were determined.

"Very well."

Mr. Guerra stepped into the rain.

I heard Sue saying to Ares, "You stay always next to me, hear me?"

"Yes, Miss Sue."

"Just Sue."

Mposi was on fire, and nobody knew who had done it.

Mr. Guerra was on the phone. "I am in."

Colonel de Mposi was ready to die, to give up.

I turned my head in every direction, looking back over my shoulder. Barracks One and Three were on fire. I lost a moment of concentration when I focused on the plaza. I saw bodies, and so did those who were with me.

"Look! Back in the plaza."

"It's about people, Mr. Rockefeller."

"Look closely, sir."

As he was about to come out of the bushland, Renita pulled him back, and I saw Alfredo and Paul crossing left, shooting, but Popo had squeezed his pistol. They fell across the muddy ground.

We stared at him.

"Where did you learn to shoot like that, Mr. Popovic?"

"I told you, Master Chief. On the Boy Scout campus."

Mr. Guerra called up again.

"I am here."

"At the plaza."

"Give me the code."

Silence.

"They caught her or the others, killed."

Mr. Guerra understood, and he had once again misunderstood Colonel de Mposi.

Concerned now, he pulled back. Renita examined the place.

From the Mposi speaker, his voice came through, mixed with the sound of the rain. "I told you, Mr. Guerra or Mr. McGowan, I am God. I know. Can you see, you and your companions are alone?"

"Mr. Rockefeller—"

"Please, sir, call me Rocko."

He looked at Ares, Popo, Witz and Ab.

Witz spoke. "He likes to be called Rocko, Master Chief."

"Alright. How many people are with him?"

"I do believe he has only Yokata, Brian and Joe with him."

"Miguel, Dieng, Ranjit, Josh?"

"Josh was dead, sir, Miguel and Ranjit as well. He killed Dieng in front of us when he refused to be part of torturing us."

"Okay," he said. "Can we move them?"

"We are in."

Renita looked at her daughter, and she nodded.

"Let's go."

"What about us?"

"We can't lose you guys. You're very precious."

Sue approached Ares and handed him a pistol. "I will take him."

"Is that a good idea, La?"

"Yes, Mum. I'll be calmer if he is next to me."

We were alert, and amidst the sounds of projectiles and Colonel de Mposi challenging Mr. Guerra and Renita, I told Ab, Witz and Popo, "This is a trap."

"How do you know?"

"I don't know, I just feel it."

"We can't trust him."

"What are we going to do, Rocko?"

"Let us burn the cottages and get Mr. de Mposi's attention."

"Shh," Witz exclaimed. "Can you hear it?"

We paid attention to the rain. The sound was coming from somewhere, and we were targeted by Yokata and Brian.

"I heard it."

"Footsteps."

I led them to the right, which gave us access to the culvert, to the brook.

We saw Yokata and Brian come to the canal like reptiles and toss themselves into the water. Brian had a problem that had nothing to do with us. He jumped forward and at the same time he cursed himself but moved as far as he could towards the opposite side, where Yokata was.

"What is the matter?"

"Something has caught me."

"Can you move?"

He was suddenly looking weary. Yokata asked him once more. Brian reached the muddy edge. He told him he could not feel his leg. When Yokata asked if he needed any help, he snapped, "Do I look like I need help?"

Brian was sure this behavior didn't make sense to Yokata, who was trying to assist him. His face changed drastically.

"Suit yourself. I go this way. You go that away."

Yokata changed his mind.

We thought we were at the right spot as Yokata began to move on. Brian could not.

"We can help him."

"Rocko, please. You heard him when the man asked him."

"A poisonous insect has bitten him."

For a moment, we were distracted, as Brian's destiny was completely in our hands. I tried to tell Popo, Ab and Witz that we were not like them.

"Please, guys."

There was the sound of a bullet. We ran along the canal. We did not have any choice but to get in. I peeked at Brian, leaning back. He had become black.

He looked at us, gesturing to his rifle, shouting, "Get down! Get down!"

"We here to help you, fool," Witz said.

"Get down!"

We continued running to his spot, until we understood his command; he raised the rifle and pulled the trigger. A bullet reached Yokata, and my own reaction was, *Why? No, no. But Yokata kept moving even though he had a bullet in his body.*

Popo pointed the pistol at Yokata. Ab, Witz and I reached Brian. As a result of whatever he had stumbled on, he had developed purple marks on his face.

"Ab, can we save him?"

"We can't, Rocko."

Brian burbled, "I can't see and I am unable to imagine."

We stared at him, helpless. After all, it would take more than a day to let a medicine man see him. He died with his eyes open.

We walked carefully to the cottages. Since we had arrived here, we hadn't heard any voices, but here and there we heard the sounds of bullets until we saw Renita and Ares on the ground.

"What happened?"

"They have been shot. I need to get my medical tools."

"Where is Mr. Guerra?"

"He went after Colonel de Mposi. This Joe is dead back there."

Suddenly, a traffic of people emerged from that side of the gully.

"Look! Look! It's Big and Eyes."

A car leaped over the pond. Behind the wheel, I saw Colonel de Mposi.

"Oh, no."

"Rocko! Rocko! Where are you going?"

"I won't let him get away."

"Take it. You can cut him across the culvert."

With a flash, I caught her handgun out of the air. I was afraid, running through the infected water and on the muddy ground, that maybe I would fall into holes; I followed the marks made by the tires of the truck. I began to feel that Mr. Mposi, in the course of his panicked, reckless drive through the jungle, would eventually fall below or die trying, and I saw then a Jeep that was moving blindly and then Mr. Guerra, whose driving was crazy and dangerous. I prayed there would be no falls, despite the fact that I did not see any hope; I saw the Jeep crash against Colonel de Mposi's truck, sending it off balance. That is to say, the truck hit a tree, and turned over. Colonel de Mposi's body flew through the window and splashed into a stream. Rain and water from the lake had combined to become a sea of water.

I couldn't see him come up.

As I became aware of that, I headed to the Jeep. Mr. Guerra was struggling inside the Jeep but was all right.

"Where is he?"

"He fell in the stream."

"Get him."

I jogged to the stream, and it was deep, as its water, actively and strongly, flowed to the river. There was a waterfall below. Rain had stopped, but it began again. Without thinking, I dived. My vision blurred. Big fish. Snakes moved away. Eels swarmed below. I paid attention to the body and grasped it, pulling it out of the water, because, as I saw that Colonel de Mposi was unconscious. It was a herculean task, but I could do it.

On the shore, I saw Witz, Big, Eyes, Sue and these uniformed men, but my effort was not over yet. I gave first aid to this man who deserved to be dead.

He coughed and water came out of his body, and he stared at me.

"You again, uh?"

"I want you to live and be punished for what you have done."

An impressive woman escorted by a dozen officers approached us.

"Is this Colonel de Mposi?"

"Yes, ma'am."

"Take him away." Then she looked at me. "I presume I am talking with Mr. Rockefeller, Jr."

"You presume right."

"Your father and other kids are Rio de Janeiro. They are waiting..."

Chapter 56

More than two military helicopters had landed in the middle of the plaza of Mposi. Officers and helpers guided the kids onboard. I was unable to see Master Chief "Steven McGowan" Guerra, Renita "Melanie Leyva" Borzaga, or her daughter, Sue, from this point onwards but they got all the boxes, Trast's confession and the way Frank Migliaro had died.

In the helicopter, Ares and the others were quiet. None of us spoke during the ten hours of flying to the American military base in Panama.

After they assisted us with the medical examination, we had a moment of relaxation, then a cross-examination, and finally, they let us into a spacious area where our mothers and fathers were waiting.

The officer read my name.

"Mr. Rockefeller, your son is here."

"He's there, sir."

I saw no arrogance on his face, but only sadness and fear. He stood before me and then, slowly, he brought me to his chest. He squeezed me, and I heard him crying.

"Dad."

He withdrew from me, and before me was a father I did not know. I did not know this side of him.

"I thought I had lost you, boy."

He kissed me and hugged me once.

The End...